The GOLDEN TABLET

BY **MILENA**

THE FIRST PART

1. INT. MILO UNDERGROUND BASE ON TARRA – DAY

A moderately lit meeting room, bare of furniture except for a table with 7 chairs. Seated along this table are 5 men and 2 women of the Milo's Committee-On-Site.

All wear dark GREY uniform-style clothes.

Their heads sparkle, revealing their brain activity. To escape that glare, they keep both of their upper eyelids quite low and mostly look down.

CHAIRPERSON

Esteemed members of this Milo Committee-On-Site, we are here today to reach important strategic decisions regarding two of our projects.

The first is the project "Globe", focused on our intention to create a brand new planet – starting from a piece of clay.

With success in this project, we will become more independent and potentially spread our civilization to many new locations.

The only obstacle is that we need galactic permission for the location of our new planet; which is not easy to obtain, bearing in mind that we do not whole-heartedly stick to the Laws of the Universe. Though the Galactic

Assembly discussed our proposal, no location has been granted yet.

MILO PERSON 7

Why would we depend on their permission?

CHAIRPERSON

Precisely. Faced with this obstacle of uncertain outcome, we suggest that we focus on a prompt finalization of one of our old and ongoing projects, Project Mélange.

You are aware that for a long time, as we were cruising across the galaxy, we have been collecting the samples of inhabitants from all the planets we visited. We have thus gathered DNA samples of three young males and three young females from those planets.

All the collected data and this entire project is kept here, inside Tarra.

MILO PERSON 6

Have we collected the samples from Tarra?

CHAIRPERSON

On Tarra, we obtained the data from two couples only.

MILO PERSON 5 (FEMALE)

Where would Project Mélange be located?

CHAIRPERSON

The initial plan was to create a new planet – and the Globe Project was to provide it.

All collected planetary representatives of Project Mélange would live together there, and we will observe how those different races harmonise with one another and how long it will take them to either create a peaceful society or to destroy themselves.

We have been in a position to notice that the most crucial challenge of each civilization has been to find a way for the peaceful coexistence of all individuals and groups, and to work for the betterment of all. That challenge is even bigger when a planet is populated by different races.

MILO PERSON 4

Sure, it is. However, challenges and uncertainties are a part of every project. The Milo civilization should remain enthusiastic about the whole experiment. We hope that the next step from that project is the creation of a new and superior race.

MILO PERSON 7

Due to the given circumstances, do we really need to waste our time by sticking to the initial plan of locating Mélange on a new planet.

CHAIRPERSON

We do not. Our team has already calculated that it is faster and easier to depopulate Tarra and to inhabit its developed surface structures with our mixed civilizations' group, than to locate our experimental group on a brand new planet. We therefore suggest that we vote for the latest proposal from our techno-specialists' team:

Ladies and gentlemen, on this E-35 date of Tarra calendar, do you agree with starting Project Mélange on the surface of Tarra?

Five hands raise up (persons 1, 4, 5, 6 and 7).

CHAIRPERSON (CONT'D)

Thank you, ladies and gentlemen. Since five, out of seven, are in favour of eliminating the Tarra's over-ground civilization, the decision is made. Looking at the voting results shows that we are making this decision with some hesitation, I would guess due to the collateral damage it implies.

However, I am glad the majority has voted in support of this project, which strives to create a civilization far better than the one currently living on the surface of Tarra. Our technical team will go through the necessary details and draft a conclusive strategy, the validity of which is effectively in power from today's Committee decision.

2.   EXT. SPACE

Inter-Galactic mothership, MANNA-373, glides through the boundless tranquillity of space.

We hear a conversation of ship CAPTAIN URROS (early 50s, tall athletic body; uncompromising yet soft in applying his authority) with young cadet FARO (late 20s, a simple and direct personality).

CAPTAIN URROS (O.S.)

We are aware that the planet Tarra is heading towards a critical stage.

FARO (O.S.)

Has the Golden Tablet been found on Tarra?

CAPTAIN URROS (O.S.)

According to our latest scanning, NO, not yet.

FARO (O.S.)

If they do not find it, what would that mean?

CAPTAIN URROS (O.S)

Unfortunately, one planetary civilization less on our charts.

3.   INT. SPACESHIP MANNA-373, FARO'S
      WORKSTATION – DAY

Faro's workstation is semicircular, made of translucent material that shimmers with internal glow.

The desk itself is responsive to touch, thought or vibration; it is a reactive interface, projecting holograms, data streams and cosmic maps directly above its surface.

There is no clatter on the surface; with very few buttons or levers; no keyboards separated from the table – commands are mostly issued via neural resonance or subtle hand gestures.

This desk is more than just a workstation. It's a symbiotic extension of the user's consciousness, designed to harmonize intellect, emotion and awareness. It reshapes itself based on task – flattening for drafting, curving for immersive simulations, or splitting into modular zones for collaboration.

Faro and Captain Urros are standing by Faro's desk and whaching a holographic rendering of the planet Tarra located above the surface of the desk.

We notice a geometric sunflower logo on their uniforms.

Patiently and eloquently, Captain Urros withstands Faro's unending curiosity.

                          FARO

        Do we know what is written in the
        Golden Tablet?

CAPTAIN URROS

We don't. But if we want to know,
we can find it in our Archive, where
the contents of all Golden Tablets
are stored. As a matter of fact, we
expect the latest report on Tarra any
moment.

A nearby beeping interrupts the conversation.

CAPTAIN URROS (CONT'D)

Let us hear what this information is
about!

*Captain Urros gets close to the beeping instrument
and presses a button. Faro follows him. Both listen.*

FEMALE NARRATOR (V.O.)

Planet Tarra (coordinates: G4, 6th
Solar System, Orbit 3). The latest
scanning results reveal a slight
decrease in planetary frequency.
If this trend, still unknown to the
residents of the planet, is not
stopped, it will be detrimental to the
entire civilisation on Tarra.

FARO

Frequency decrease! Are we allowed
to help the Tarran people?

CAPTAIN URROS

Yes, and we have always been doing
so within the parameters prescribed.

In the forthcoming planetary
catastrophes, which the populace

might not even be aware of, the Golden Tablet is also there to help. It carries the salvation programme. Once found, it will be the tool to lead Tarra to safety. However, the Tarran people will have to do their homework.

CENTER: FARO

Was Tarra not a stable planet!?

CENTER: CAPTAIN URROS

Time will tell. If you press the planets button here, you will find general information about Tarra. By the way, WELCOME to our MANNA-373 crew.

4.   INT. SPACESHIP MANNA-373 – DAY

Seated comfortably, Faro puts an ear peace on.

His finger presses the "planets" button. He chooses "Tarra".

Video begins. We watch about:

TARRA

PLANET TARRA is nested in an energy bubble. ENTERING that bubble reveals TARRA's planetary zones: a wide equatorial section occupied with seven distinctive hexagonal continents; North and South polar hexagonal caps each surrounded by a Polar Lake; a forest area connecting Polar Lakes with the continental masses.

All but one continent appear painted with a different colour: Continent 1 – red, 2 – orange, 3 – yellow, 4 – green, 5 – a mixture of colours, 6 – indigo, 7 – purple.

These colours are moderately present on house facades, street and pathway surfaces, but are DOMINANT on ANIMALS and ALL FOLIAGE.

Following the hexagonal shape of each continent, town planning and landscaping are organised through a hexagonal fractality. In the very centre of each continent is a huge hexagonal Square (the Central Square), with a massive pyramidal-type building in the middle (the six-sided Central Pyramid).

This building is the major continental landmark. Its very top is made of transparent material, tinted into the colour dominant on the given continent. On Continent 1 it provides a reddish ambient, Continent 2 – orange, etc.

There are three entrances to the Pyramid (one on every other side). They are each a huge opening without a door. An extremely big number above the entrances marks the name of that continent (1, 2, 3, 4, 5, 6 or 7).

The hexagonal floor of the Pyramid cascades into an audience space, with seven mildly-steep steps down from the entrance level. A wide corridor encircles that section.

Each Central Square also has a Monument – the same on all seven continents. It is a giant model of Tarra that features its topography. The globe is pierced by its vertical axis, extended high up to hold Tarra's flag.

In the middle of the flag is a PURPLE HEXAGON, presented on the top of FIVE horizontal colour stripes of equal size. Colours from bottom to the top are: red, orange, yellow, green and indigo.

On each continent, there is a network of streets and pedestrian paths leading to parks, lakes, forests and colourful meadows.

Water is an integral part of the ambience – indoor and outdoor. There are fountains, ponds, narrow canals alongside streets and pedestrian paths.

As we watch the above, together with the selection of images suggested by the following narration, we hear:

MALE NARRATOR (V.O.)

Tarra is populated by a humanoid race and belongs to the group of sealed planets. Not all cosmic energy can penetrate its atmosphere nor can the thought energy of Tarran citizens cruise through the celestial spheres beyond Tarra. Hence Tarran civilisation is perpetuating a status quo in consciousness, from generation to generation.

The inhabited section of Tarra is a wide equatorial belt, occupied by seven equal hexagonal continents, each named by a number.

The climate on Tarra is constant with temperatures in the range of 20*C to 26*C. It rains only during the night, yet never in the manner of a storm. Tarra is abundant with plant species. The only animals that live on the planet are birds and butterflies.

Tarra has one sun, the light of which appears slightly misty.

Tarra's year lasts 343 days, and is divided into 7 months, each comprising of 49 days. The months are named by a single letter (A, B, C, D, E, F and G).

HOUSEHOLDS

In line with the hexagonal design-template of Tarra, each individual house sits on a plot composed of four joint hexagonal units.

Houses are shaped as pyramids. Their four-sided base is founded on two joint equilateral triangles. These triangles are derived by diagonals of the hexagonal plot units.

The top sections of majority of houses are transparent and can open. Internally, houses are usually organised through several floors, some of which have spacious balconies overlooking their private gardens.

Every household has their own home vehicle (pyramobile), parked within their plot of land.

All pyramobiles are identical, except for the colour design of their outer shell. They can fly and hover above the ground.

A family's plot of land is a perfectly maintained garden, surrounded by invisible energy curtains.

Only the people who dwell in a property can enter it. Others encounter an invisible energy barrier and are unable to pass through it. Hence, individual plots have no visible fences; houses are not locked.

As we watch the above, together with the selection of images suggested by the following narration, we hear:

MALE NARRATOR (V.O.)

The inhabitants of Tarra live either as a family of three (two parents and one child) or as single adults in one household.

Homes are seen as private sanctuaries, perfectly fit for their dwellers. The house scans the coordinates of all individuals in it. Guests, visiting for the first time, can only step into somebody's garden or house if accompanied by the host.

A dweller's existential needs are all met. Households are self-sufficient in every manner. Clean energy is generated naturally. Food manifests the moment it is intended and envisaged.

Internal organisation of houses is flexible. Voice instructions can make walls move, appear or disappear.

Interior OBJECTS (tables, chairs) CHANGE COLOUR in response to the thought frequency of their owner. Guests have no impact on the colour of these objects.

WORK AND LIFESTYLE

At any moment during the day there are Tarrans in nature, or their garden, focused on flowers, shrubs, trees, butterflies or birds. They draw, measure or just observe them. Piles of botanical sketches are commonly found in personal offices where studies continue.

Daily work is concluded by pressing a "DC – SEND" on the keyboard.

Tarran people love to spend time in nature, to walk, run, exercise, pursue hobbies or fly in adorable pyramobiles.

They dress in loose, comfortable, multi-layered clothes made of natural materials, the colour of which reflects the dominant colour of their continent.

As we watch the above, together with the selection of images suggested by the following narration, we hear:

MALE NARRATOR (V.O.)

The adult population are research scientists. They study the relationship of sound and colour, in particular the communication language of PLANTS, BUTTERFLIES and BIRDS. The outcome of their daily work is fed into the Diffusion Centre (DC), located at Tarra's North Pole. From this Centre, on a daily basis, data is transferred to the celestial Dimension that administers Tarra.

The input of the whole Tarra workforce is closely supervised and any necessary guidance is provided via personal files.

The majority of Tarran residents are excellent at drawing and painting, which complements their research activities. Each adult plays multiple musical instruments. The most common way of spending time together as a family is being outside in nature. All hobbies and recreation never include members of other households.

There is no collective activity of any kind, nor community buildings except the Central Pyramid.

On the planet Tarra, there is no form of government, yet a pristine order reigns. The future is not a topic on the minds of Tarran people, for their life is ruled by certainty.

MILO CIVILIZATION

Tarra also hosts the underground facilities of the MILO civilisation. Instead of hair, these humanoids have transparent skin revealing their brain currents' sparks. If they do not cover their heads, they resemble walking firework sticks.

Their two upper eyelids, each of a different thickness, can be used separately or together, depending on the environmental brightness.

Outside their facilities, when mingling through Tarran people, Milo operatives use a special cap to cover their sparkling heads.

As we watch the above, together with the selection of images suggested by the following narration, we hear:

MALE NARRATOR (V.O.)

Beside the Tarran people who live on the planetary surface, there is another civilization using the planetary interior for its

TECHNOLOGICAL BASE. It is the Milo civilization, who are known as busy interplanetary travellers.

Tarra suits them due to the stable surface environment and the docile civilization dwelling on it. The MILO are a human-looking race. The Tarran civilization on the planetary surface is unaware of them.

Faro stops the video, takes his headphones off and continues sitting, much consumed by what he has learnt about Tarra.

5.   EXT. CONTINENT 7, TIBAR'S GARDEN – DAY

This continent is dominated by the colour purple. We see the garden of a house with a captivating variety of flowers, shrubs, trees, and water features. The colour of foliage and most flowers is in the rich range of purple. The birds (generally purple feathered) are perched on branches or fly from place to place.

The garden belongs to TIBAR (male, 38; hides a great strength behind his mild face and words).

KOA (Tibar's son, soon to be 17, a young man with a disarming smile and a plethora of talents) is busy with one bird that continuously returns to him. The bird's feathers are multi-coloured, yet predominantly purple.

It seems the bird follows what Koa commands it to do. He throws a small object, the bird flies to find it and returns it to him.

Eventually, the bird sits on Koa's shoulder.

Koa walks towards the house.

6.   INT. CONTINENT 7, TIBAR'S HOUSE – DAY

Tibar is in a botanical utility room (worktop, sink with a tap, garden tools, wall shelves with neatly marked and ordered seed containers).

The yearly calendar on the worktop shows E-36, 232 (111).

E-36 is the date: month E, the day 36th of that month. 232 stands for the 232nd day of the year, while 111 indicates the number of days left to the end of the year.

Tibar looks for some seeds, finds what he wants, gets a small garden tool and walks out of this room.

At the exit to the garden, he meets Koa who is coming from the garden with the bird on his shoulder.

> TIBAR
>
> Koa, I am going to the garden to plant a new range of purple-3 tulips. Now is the right moment.

> KOA
>
> Enjoy it, father.

7.   EXT. CONTINENT 7, TIBAR'S GARDEN – DAY

Knelt on the ground, Tibar digs a hole, puts the seeds in it, covers the seeds and then convincingly yet softly tells them:

> TIBAR
>
> Soon, you are going to be the most eloquent tulips in this garden.

Tibar digs another hole. His tool hits something solid.

He digs out a tablet-shaped case made of silvery metal.

8.   INT. CONTINENT 7, TIBAR'S HOUSE – DAY

Tibar is finely cleaning the metal case in the botanical utility room, then CAREFULLY OPENS the case and finds a GOLDEN TABLET (7.6cm x 12.3cm x 1.3cm) in it.

He takes the Golden Tablet out and observes it.

On its top side is a deeply embossed hexagon divided by its diagonals into six equilateral Golden Triangles. Nothing else is on the tablet's front or back side.

9.   INT. CONTINENT 7, KOA'S ROOM – DAY

KOA

From his earliest childhood, Koa has been the boy with a sunny smile and ample joy in his voice. He is interested in vibrations, energy, frequencies, music, modelling and flying.

Koa's hobby room is a mini techno-musical-digital laboratory. It is placed on the first floor, and has a big balcony above the side of the garden where their pyramobile is parked. Koa loves spending time on balcony to watch the night sky.

Inside this room, there is a continuous worktop along two walls and wall shelves above it.

The worktop is covered by a selection of electronic equipment, other simple tools and numberless sketches – particularly of birds.

The shelves are dedicated to various sized models of birds, butterflies, interesting flying objects and robotic looking toys.

Several bigger models of flying objects, and birds with stretched wings, are hang from the ceiling.

The walls are additionally lined with posters and paintings. The posters feature musical diagrams, cymatics patterns, a GEOMETRIC ANALYSIS of the SEEDS' FORMATION on SUNFLOWER head, mathematical calculations, fractal geometries, as well as blueprints of Koa's creations.

Many musical instruments, including crystal singing bowls, a series of gongs, a keyboard, a flute, a didgeridoo, a guitar as well as tuning forks, occupy a separate part of the room.

Amongst the many toys he has made, HUMA is Koa's favourite. It is his personal companion, the performances of which he is continuously upgrading. Koa takes it with him whenever he goes outside.

When Koa utters "Huma", the bird flies to him and ends up on Koa's shoulder as a programmed location. Specific words command Huma to perform different tasks. Huma has an array of flying trajectories, wing movements, and can also hover in the air. The repertoire of its tunes, laughs, and its very vocabulary, is constantly growing.

Koa can hover above the ground. He is the only one on the planet with that skill, which his mother trained him into. He uses it only when alone, since he would not like to be seen as different.

Koa is in his room, bent over a section of his long worktop line, carefully constructing delicate clockwork toys.

Beside him is a collection of 5 platonic solids.

We hear a knocking at his door.

KOA

Yes!

Koa turns around and sees his father entering the room with a silvery object in his hand.

Tibar walks to Koa, opens the metal case, takes the Golden Tablet out and places both objects on the worktop in front of Koa.

TIBAR

Koa, look what I have just dug up in
the garden!

Koa is curious and calm. He takes the objects, one at the time, into his hands and for a good while examines them from all sides.

TIBAR (CONT'D)

As you can see, even though there is
no information on it, the Tablet has
been encased so carefully as if to be
preserved for the distant future.

Quiet for some time, still focused on both objects:

KOA

Yes. It is strange, yet I do not doubt
the Tablet is genuine and INTENDED.
I only wonder about its meaning,
since it reveals nothing of itself
except these six triangles. Look,
they might be detachable from their
hexagonal base.

Koa tries and manages to take first one and then all six Golden Triangles out.

                    TIBAR

    Why are they detachable?

                    KOA

    It is too early to know.

                    TIBAR

    I suppose.

They both hold some Triangles for a while.

Koa returns them to their place in the Golden Tablet.

                TIBAR (CONT'D)

    Isn't it peculiar, Koa, that I feel
    attracted to this BLANK TABLET. Since
    I saw it and touched it, some kind of
    anticipation was immediately born,
    suggesting a huge significance to its
    discovery.

                    KOA

    Father, I am sure time will unfold the
    mystery.

                    TIBAR

    I will keep the Tablet on my desk. You
    are welcome to visit it at any time.

Tibar places the Tablet back into its case and walks towards the door through which he came in.

Three models of four legged creatures are on the floor by that very door. Impressed with discovering them,

Tibar takes one in his hands and observes its unusual shape.

                    TIBAR (CONT'D)

When did you make these models?
What are they?

Koa turns towards the door, gets up from his chair and joins his father who holds a model of a white cat, with small black sections on its tail and ears.

                        KOA

Ah, those ones! They were made
recently after I saw them in my
dream. They are called CATS – I was
INFORMED. I was on a planet where
only cats live, of course in large
numbers and scattered throughout
lush vegetation.

                       TIBAR

Cats ruling an entire planet! SO
LITTLE DO WE KNOW!

                        KOA

True! SO LITTLE DO WE KNOW!
Unfortunately, I did not meet the
CAT, the top Governor of their plant,
to be able to tell you more.

Both smile.

                       TIBAR

I can see, you were very impressed,
you made not one but three of them.

Tibar returns the white cat to the floor and takes the ginger cat into his hands.

KOA

Yes, because I was playing with
three of them and I loved each one.
I remember, I communicated with
them – yet I do not recall how.

Tibar puts the ginger cat model back on the floor.

TIBAR

Have you given names to them?

KOA

Yes. That one is Rory, the white one is
Romy and the black one is Rocco.

10.   INT. MILO UNDERGROUND BASE – DAY

Technical group meeting of three Milo operatives.

OPERATIVE 1

In order to most successfully deploy
our frequency reduction programme
on Tarra, we have to deal with a
particular technical element.

The Diffusion Centre (DC), located
at Tarra's North Pole, does not
only harvest the data of the daily
work of the Tarran people. It also
continuously adjusts the frequency of
the entire population. The frequency
is kept in a range necessary to make
people carry on with their work, and

be contented within the planetary social order.

Cosmic influences are disabled, and the whole planet is subject to the frequency dictum of this Diffusion Centre.

What we need to do is to REPROGRAM the frequency range, making sure not to affect the daily work data collection. Once we do that, our influence on the planetary crystalline grid will produce results much quicker. Any questions?

OPERATIVE 2

What about the personnel at the Centre?

OPERATIVE 1

To our knowledge, the Diffusion Centre is fully remotely operated, yet we do not have any details about the security system they employ. Any other questions?

No questions.

OPERATIVE 1 (CONT'D)

Thanks. See you tonight.

11.   INT. CONTINENT 7, TIBAR'S HOUSE – DAY

The deep sound of a gong floods the entire house then starts receding.

We see Koa in his room move away from a huge free standing gong towards a collection of crystal singing bowls on the floor.

He sits on the floor getting himself ready to play them. Just before the last vibration of the gong dies out, the relaxing sound of the crystal bowls spreads across the house.

12.   INT. CONTINENT 7, TIBAR'S ROOM – DAY

Tibar is busy working in his ground-floor home office that resembles a compact bio-laboratory. He is organising the measurements obtained from outdoors.

Sounds from the singing bowls enter his room and take him to the time when Koa was young and his mother VERA (profound, discreet and lovable personality) was still on the planet.

He stops his work and succumbs to memories.

We follow four of these recalls.

13.   INT. CONTINENT 7, KOA'S ROOM – DAY (FLASHBACK)

Vera plays the crystal bowls. Young Koa (6 years old) beside her, tries to imitate what mom is doing.

14.   EXT. CONTINENT 7, MEADOW – DAY (FLASHBACK)

A happy family runs through a flowery meadow.

They laugh, chase one another, play with a ball.

15.   EXT. CONTINENT 7, TIBAR'S GARDEN – DAY (FLASHBACK)

Laying on the purplish grass in his garden, Tibar adjusts measuring instruments attached to the stalks of neighbouring roses.

Vera and Koa are coming. Koa is curious about his father's activity.

KOA

(voice of a child)

What are you doing, father?

TIBAR

Trying to understand what one rose
tells to another?

KOA

(voice of a child)

Why don't you ask butterflies?

16.   INT. CONTINENT 7, KOA'S ROOM – DAY (FLASHBACK)

The whole family is gathered around a huge canvas placed on the floor.

Each one of them loads a brush with paint and makes some brush strokes in turn.

Occasionally, Tibar takes Koa in his hands and helps him hover above the canvas, in order to splash the paint to more central parts of the canvas.

The painting is finished.

Tibar, Vera and Koa are cheering.

Full view of that painting.

17.   INT. CONTINENT 7, KOA'S ROOM – DAY

Full view of that painting, this time hanging on the wall in Koa's room.

Koa is still playing the crystal bowls.

He stops and walks towards the door.

18.   INT. CONTINENT 7, TIBAR'S ROOM – DAY

Koa enters in his father's office room. His father is sitting, deeply in thought.

                    KOA

          Father, I was thinking to ask you
          something for a long time.

                    TIBAR

          What is it, Koa?

                    KOA

          I love our pyramobile, even its name
          OMNIA. I have been thinking to ask
          your permission to fly it.

For a moment, he stops talking to observe father's reaction. Tibar does not show any.

                    KOA (CONT'D)

          You know how much I enjoy studying
          the physics of flight? I watched you

pilot Omnia for years. I could build a working model of a pyramobile blindfolded!

I know that officially, you must be 18 to fly a pyramobile... but please... father. Please, consider letting me fly now!? Even just short patrols around the house! Anything!

TIBAR

I see. I am not really surprised with what I am hearing.

OK. I will grant you my permission under two conditions. Firstly – we do three flights together, with me co-piloting to test your skills. Secondly – if you pass, you fly during the night only since traffic is less frequent then.

KOA

Excellent! I will wait for you to call me for my first piloting session.

19.   INT. OMNIA, CONTINENT 7 – DAY

Tibar and Koa with Huma are inside Omnia.

Tibar shows Koa around, explaining each instrument on the dashboard.

Koa follows attentively, sometimes asking questions. We do not hear this conversation, but we understand it from their body language.

Eventually, they both sit down and Koa takes off on his first time piloting Omnia. The flight is smooth.

Through the window, occasionally Tibar admires the view of their continent.

Huma is on the windowsill close to Koa.

TIBAR

How does it feel?

KOA

Even better than I thought.

At that instant, Huma utters a rather unpleasant sound, like a sudden warning, indicating an out-of-ordinary frequency.

Omnia shakes, bounces off and makes a slight shift in direction.

Tibar and Koa rush to check all instruments on the dashboard.

TIBAR

All is under control. We hit the
protective energy curtain of our
continent, hence were redirected.
It was not dangerous because the
entrance angle of the collision was
very acute.

Despite the unpleasant surprise, Tibar continues as a reputable teacher.

TIBAR (CONT'D)

Koa, did you know that every
continent on Tarra is surrounded
with its own energetic curtains that

stop the entrance of vehicles from neighbouring continents?

KOA

I have noticed we would always fly above our continent, but now I see it was not just your choice. So, people cannot leave their continent. Why?

TIBAR

This planet does not exist to solely host our life here. Tarra is a research laboratory. Energetic zones are clearly defined to provide a variety of controlled environments to the living species that we study. It is about the energy hygiene necessary for our scientific advancement – not about our freedom. One can always redefine freedom. Isn't it?

KOA

I see.

TIBAR

Have you noticed that we never fly far North, nor far South?

KOA

Yes. I have, though have never understood why.

TIBAR

It is related to the energy of the planet. There is an intensification of the magnetic field as one approaches the magnetic poles.

We can fly, land, and then walk outside our pyramobiles only up to the 66th parallel, of both South and North hemispheres. If we land, let us say at the 69th parallel, we will not be able to comfortably function or even walk out there.

20.   INT. CONTINENT 7, TIBAR'S ROOM – DAY

A quiet atmosphere in Tibar's office room. Next to the window is a desk with the Golden Tablet on it.

Tibar is sitting by the desk and writing in his diary.

We follow his fountain pen moving across the page: "Tarra has seven continents!

The Tablet has six Triangles!? Where is the connection, if any? May I not to be late in understanding. I must, I want, I will succeed!".

He underlines the last sentence.

21.   INT. CONTINENT 7, TIBAR'S ROOM – DAY

Another day. The same scene, yet, to Tibar, the colours inside the room are slightly different from those of the previous day.

Tibar's hand finishes the sentence: "I must, I want, I will succeed".

Slowly, he puts the fountainpen aside and closes the diary.

22.   INT. SMALL MILO SPACESHIP – NIGHT

Three Milo operatives are inside their spaceship flying towards Tarra's North Pole. They are getting close to the Diffusion Centre (DC).

Gradually, on their screen, a spacious single level hexagonal building, tightly surrounded by the waters of the North Polar Lake, emerges through the darkness of the night.

There are six tall antenna-like pillars on each hexagon's corner.

The roof of the building is the only possible place to land. Its centre is engraved with a hexagon (about 5 metres wide), featuring a logo in the middle.

23.   EXT. DIFFUSION CENTRE – NIGHT

The Milo spaceship comfortably lands on the roof of the Diffusion Centre.

Three operatives step out, all equipped with backpacks and dressed in dark grey wetsuit-looking garments. Their heads are covered by tight caps with an added torch at their foreheads.

They come to the roof edge and circle around it, intending to find a way down or an indication of the building's entrance. Even though they have walked around the entire roof, they do not find what they are looking for.

Each operative takes equipment from his backpack, fixes ropes against the roof and abseils down approximately five metres to reach the ground.

Their soft boots touch the narrow pavement that separates the building from the Polar Lake.

Carefully, they walk around the building looking for the door.

There are no doors.

Three Milo operatives are not giving up, yet they do not utter a word.

Perfectly trained, each one of them takes a special piece of equipment from his backpack, and they spread around the building to scan the outside walls.

They check the entire building, then meet up together.

OPERATIVE 1

The wall is evenly thick all around the building.

A new tool emerges from their backpacks and is soon applied to cut the wall with a beam of light.

All three work together on making an entrance through the many-layered and very thick external wall.

24.   INT. DIFFUSION CENTRE – NIGHT

Three Milo operatives enter the Diffusion Centre through the opening in the wall, which they have just made.

The interior is dark and resembles a futuristic apartment. The central part is a spacious hexagonal open space, with the character of a living room. The receding cascades of its ceiling follow the same hexa-geometry.

As the operatives spread around the building looking for any sign of technology, the lights switch on.

One of the operatives discovers a computer room. He steps inside and walks towards the computers.

At that instant, a part of the wall, that looks like a built-in piece of technological equipment, detaches, revealing a well-camouflaged robot that swiftly moves and charges towards the Milo operative. A battle between the two starts.

With the activation of one robot, five other robots camouflaged in different parts of the building are automatically triggered and start patrolling. The battle escalates.

The Milo team of operatives gradually outrivals the robots. As they move the battlefield out of the computer room, one operative installs their computer programme and completes what they came to do.

25.   INT. CONTINENT 7, TIBAR'S ROOM – NIGHT

Tibar sits by his desk and observes the Golden Tablet.

The room door is open.

KOA

Are you there, father?

TIBAR

Yes! Yes, I am.

KOA

Father, as I have passed my flying
test, I am getting myself ready for my
first solo flight tonight. See you in the
morning.

TIBAR

Be careful, Koa.

KOA

Of course. How else?

26. INT. OMNIA, CONTINENT 7 – NIGHT

Koa and Huma are inside Omnia. Koa is piloting southwards from their house.

KOA

Huma, do you remember what my father said about the 66th parallel? Let's check it out!

The bird responds with the manner of a slightly mechanical voice:

HUMA

Let's check it out!

Omnia glides effortlessly through the night sky. Koa monitors the control panels.

His eyes are focused on the latitude indicator. Omnia passes the 66th – 67th – 68th – 69th – 70th parallels.

At the 76th South parallel, the Great Forest ends, touching the waters of the Polar Lake. Omnia lands.

27. EXT. CONTINENT 7, 76TH PARALLEL – NIGHT

Darkness saturated with silence.

With Huma, Koa slowly steps out of Omnia. He takes some tentative testing steps, carefully observing the entire experience.

As he feels unaffected, he moves on and finds a spot to enjoy the view: a starry sky and the mirror-like surface of the enormous Polar Lake.

KOA

Look at this sky! What an immensity of distances and mysteries! Who lives there? Huma, would we ever know?

Huma picks up a new frequency and is humming an electronic-type tune.

Koa is immersed in the beauty of the moment.

As he looks at the horizon, a disk-like flying object appears nearly touching the horizon, then immediately disappears into Tarra's interior (the UFO is visible only when very close to the ground).

KOA (CONT'D)

Did you see that, Huma? You would not believe it!

Koa makes some up-and-down steps and occasionally looks at the horizon.

KOA (CONT'D)

Maybe it was my imagination? I am not sure now.

Huma moves to Koa and lands on his open palm. Koa brings Huma to his eye height and suggests:

KOA (CONT'D)

Let us sit for a while to see whether
the vehicle will come out!

HUMA

Let us sit.

*Huma resumes his electronic-type tune. Time passes.
Koa waits for the UFO to reappear, but to no avail.*

Huma's tune gradually dissolves into silence.

KOA

We shall come again, Huma. Now we
go!

28.   INT. OMNIA, CONTINENT 7 AND 6 – NIGHT

*Koa flies back home in Omnia over his continent. He
has just seen a UFO entering Tarra. Excited, yet slightly
confused, he has so much on his mind.*

KOA

What a night, Huma!

*Instead of an ear-pleasing response, a warning sound
bursts out of Huma's beak.*

Omnia shakes slightly and continues on its course.

*Koa checks the command board, then reaches Huma
and lifts its left wing high up.*

*The wing in that position gives access to a small wing-
like cover.*

*Koa lifts that cover up to find the information he is
looking for. He reads the frequency.*

He then looks at the dashboard and makes a comparison.

KOA (CONT'D)

Huma, you are right. This is not the
frequency of our continent. We
are flying over the neighbouring
Continent 6.

He double checks the frequency figures.

KOA (CONT'D)

Yes. It is Continent 6. But according
to father, that was not possible
because of the protective energy
curtains. He also said that we cannot
exit our pyramobile beyond the 66th
parallel. What is going on?

He looks at Huma, as if asking for guidance.

HUMA

What is going on?

KOA

Huma, let's NOT wander above
Continent 6 now. We had enough
surprise for one night. We will do it
some other time. Actually, not only
that. If the continental curtains are
penetrable, we can now explore all
other continents.

The bird's mechanical voice responds:

HUMA

All continents. Some other time.

29. EXT. CONTINENT 7, TIBAR'S GARDEN – NIGHT

Another night. It rains slightly. Koa with Huma walks towards Omnia.

> KOA
>
> What do you think, Huma, are we going to see the UFO again?

> HUMA
>
> Are we?

> KOA
>
> It is ME who is asking! Not you.

Koa smiles and strokes Huma gently.

They enter Omnia.

30. EXT. CONTINENT 7, GREAT FOREST – NIGHT

Mysterious darkness covered by a starry sky. At a comfortable spot, Koa sits looking over the tranquil Polar Lake, fully focused on the horizon. He does not wait long to see a UFO heading inside Tarra.

> KOA
>
> Huma! IT IS REAL! I was not imagining!

Koa jumps up in excitement, then looks to the sky and utterly humbled sends words to it:

> KOA (CONT'D)
>
> THANK YOU!

Then, he turns to Huma.

KOA (CONT'D)

But, Huma, do not ask me to whom I
say "thank you". I would not be able
to explain.

31. EXT. CONTINENT 7, TIBAR'S HOUSE – NIGHT

*Tibar is sitting by his desk in his room. He occasionally
holds the Golden Tablet in his hands then his diary – as
if comparing the two.*

*As he hears the announcement ("Omnia landing"),
from the pyramobile info board placed inside the main
entrance to the house, Tibar hurries to meet Koa.*

Soon, Koa with Huma enters the house.

KOA

Hi, father. I thought you were
sleeping.

TIBAR

Actually, I did not even try. Did you
have a good flight?

KOA

Oh yes, the stars were so bright. But,
is everything ok with you? Why are
you waiting for me?

TIBAR

Everything is fine. More than that:
I am so thrilled. I could not wait to
share something with you.

KOA

You shall tell me all about it, after a
good night's rest.

32. EXT. CONTINENT 7, TIBAR'S GARDEN – DAY

Tibar is in his garden checking a flower bed.

He holds a piece of paper in his hand.

Koa joins him.

KOA

Father, don't you think that the
flowers in our garden are recently
not doing that great?

TIBAR

I am afraid, you are right. But I have
not been able to identify the reason.

KOA

There is something you wanted to
share with me?

TIBAR

Yes.

*They walk slowly towards the garden chairs and sit
there.*

TIBAR (CONT'D)

You are aware of the Golden Tablet
that I excavated on the E-36 day, and
that it is blank on both sides.

From that day, I left it on my desk, out of its case, so that I could see it all the time. I have also started to record my thoughts, inspired by the Tablet.

Koa is all ears.

We watch a visual illustration of the following recall:

TIBAR (CONT'D, O.S.)

Yesterday morning, I was in my room standing by the open window enjoying the morning sunshine.

Then I moved towards my desk, to place some thoughts in my diary. While I was approaching the desk, I noticed some kind of purplish light play above the Tablet.

As the sun was shining stronger, the vibrating light solidified into purple lines and letters on the Tablet. I managed to control my excitement enough to copy what I saw on the Tablet – just in case I never see it again.

KOA

Incredible! Well done, father! And what happened today when the sun entered the room?

TIBAR

There is nothing on the Tablet today. Even yesterday it turned blank, as soon as the sunlight was gone.

KOA

Now I understand why I did not see
you yesterday at all. Can I see the
copy you have made?

TIBAR

Here it is.

*Tibar hands over to Koa the paper with a copy of the
Tablet's inscription.*

Koa looks at it carefully and reads out loud:

KOA

"THINGS CAN CHANGE IN BOTH
DIRECTIONS.

TIME IS SCARCE. TARRA SHOULD
VIBRATE IN UNISON

AND LIVE IN JOY AS ONE. BELIEVE
AND ENDEAVOUR."

TIBAR

Is it not that Tarra already lives in
peace and unity?

KOA

There might be more to unity than
what we live on this planet!

TIBAR

Besides, I do my daily job diligently
and so do the others – is it not a joy?

KOA

Joy is when each of our cells is singing one tune. It is not less than bliss – one frequency in a unison of billions.

TIBAR

How is that possible?

Only a smile from Koa.

TIBAR (CONT'D)

If the Tablet is of planetary importance, then why has it been given to me? – As if I am extra capable of acting upon it! Besides, maybe, each garden has one Tablet, and perhaps even with different messages? How can I know the truth? As a single person, how can I answer to this mysterious challenge?

KOA

You are not alone, father. You have me... and Huma.

TIBAR

Thank you, son. Good to be aware of it. I do not want to mislead people, but how can I be sure that I am not making a mistake in my approach and interpretation of the Tablet?

KOA

By sticking to your essence and its guidance.

TIBAR

What do you mean?

KOA

We are BEINGS that are bigger
than our thinking mind, which can
often confuse us. We have a chance
to discover the essence-self and
integrate with it.

TIBAR

What ESSENCE-SELF?

KOA

The one that is prompting you to do
something now, regarding the Tablet.

TIBAR

True. I feel something like an inner
command. It tells me that I MUST
travel and find like-minded people, in
order to solve this mystery and help
the planet. So, I will take a time off,
and you are free to join me.

KOA

Thank you, father. I cannot wait.

TIBAR

But how can we leave our continent?
How can we enter other continents?

KOA

I would not worry about it, father,
but focus on upholding your

commitment. I need to see the original Tablet again before we depart.

Still holding the paper copy of the Tablet's content, Koa points to five lines encircling the hexagon.

KOA (CONT'D)

What do you think about these five lines and the triangles scattered on them?

TIBAR

I am still thinking.

33. INT. CONTINENT 7, TIBAR'S ROOM – DAY

Koa is in his father's room. He is sitting by the desk with the Golden Tablet on it.

Lots of measuring devices surround him.

Koa uses them to examine the Golden Tablet and its six Triangles.

THE SECOND PART

34. EXT. CONTINENT 7, TIBAR'S GARDEN – DAY

The main door of Tibar's house seen from the garden.

Tibar opens the door and steps out.

Koa follows with Huma cheerfully flying around.

Father and son walk towards Omnia and board it. Thus their journey begins.

35. INT. OMNIA, CONTINENTS 7 AND 1 – DAY

Omnia takes off with Tibar, Koa and Huma on board.

Through the window, we see their house fading away.

Koa is piloting.

Tibar has much on his mind.

                    KOA

Father, I am proud of you.

                    TIBAR

How come?

                    KOA

You have already overcome one of
the mental barriers – the fear of the
unknown!

                    TIBAR

Have I?

                    KOA

Yes, you have. Starting this journey
shows that your commitment to a
higher cause is stronger than the fear
from uncertainties or even failure.
Can you not see how amazing you
are, father?

                    TIBAR

Oh, Koa! But some other fears are
still popping up in my mind.

I do not remember being aware
of them before the Golden Tablet
appeared in my life.

KOA

Father, shall we make an agreement
– do not fear the fears that are in
your mind. They are just a mental
construct. Acknowledge them and
stop investing a single thought on
them. Otherwise, it will be like
feeding the beast who can eventually
eat you.

TIBAR

I understand. That is what I am slowly
realising as well, as I sharpen my self-
observation.

KOA

Fantastic!

TIBAR

Yes, it is. But it is not easy.

KOA

Of course, you are REORGANISING
THE MANAGEMENT of your
THOUGHTS and ATTENTION.
It requires an AWAKENED and
DISCIPLINED MIND.

Instead of throwing your precious
thought energy into the abyss of
fear, you use it to build something

of lasting value – and that is a
STRONGER and BETTER SELF.

                    TIBAR

Koa, as I listen to you, in moments,
I have an impression as if your dear
mother is speaking to me. You are so
much like her.

                    KOA

Strange, you said that. All these years
since she is not on Tarra with us, I
feel her presence very often.

I would not be surprised that she is
cheering both of us on, right now.

*Father and son sink into silence filled with emotions
and memories.*

*As they continue their journey, they graciously take
their past with them.*

                    TIBAR

Don't you have any fear related to
this journey?

                    KOA

I have a slight concern, which I would
not consider a fear. It is to do with
the fact that we have no concrete
plan regarding this journey we are
starting.

                    TIBAR

Koa, at present, I only know that I
could no longer stay at home and

continue dreaming about realising
the planetary mission.

"BELIEVE AND ENDEAVOUR" – says
the Tablet. Does it not? This message
makes me stronger and proactive.

Huma utters one of his warning sounds.

*Father and son are too consumed in their conversation
to notice it.*

TIBAR (CONT'D)

I have been thinking a lot about
the Tablet since it entered my life.
The more I was thinking, the more
I was creating a labyrinth that was
imprisoning and paralysing me. Then
I turned to common sense, and found
the CLARITY and the WILL to proceed
through concrete action – which is
this journey.

Something is reassuring me that the
necessary steps, or what we could
call a plan, will gradually unfold from
circumstances created along the way.
Actually, MY ENTIRE BEING is telling
me that it cannot even be any other
way at this moment. Does this make
sense?

KOA

I see your point. You are a vision
holder, father. So, HOLD YOUR
VISION AND BELIEF! We need that
background energy.

TIBAR

Thanks for your support. It makes
it easier for me to leave behind the
comfort of our daily life. By the way,
you need to rest, Koa. Let me fly!

Koa moves from the pilot's position.

Tibar takes over and examines the data on dashboard.

TIBAR (CONT'D)

(surprised, nearly panicking)

We are not flying above our
continent! We are over Continent 1!
So, IT IS POSSIBLE?

Huma utters the same tune as he did moments ago.

KOA

Thanks, Huma. We could have paid
better attention to your observations.

In contrast to his father, Koa is calm and unsurprised.

KOA (CONT'D)

For some reasons, obviously, the
magnetic curtains around the
continent are not as strong as before.

TIBAR

Here we are then! The first direction
on this mysterious journey has just
been revealed. Let us land on this
continent!

KOA

Are we taking the Golden Tablet set
with us?

TIBAR

I would rather leave it in Omnia.

36.   EXT. CONTINENT 1, STREET – DAY

The dominant colours on this continent are in the range of red hues.

Father and son, dressed in purple robes, walk in cheerful anticipation of something special awaiting them here. They are passing some residential dwellings.

Huma flies well ahead of them, eager to explore new territories.

When father and son reach Huma, they see an older woman (TYRA) sitting in front of her house and smiling to passers-by.

Huma is perched on her shoulder singing one of its most pleasant tunes.

KOA

Hi, I am Koa – the owner of this bird.
I hope it did not disturb you? This is
my father, Tibar.

TYRA

No, not at all. The bird is a great
companion. Pleased to meet you.

Koa takes Huma from Tyra.

TIBAR

We are traveling through this
continent, actually, we have just
started. Would you perhaps have a
recommendation or a guidance?

TYRA

Welcome. My name is Tyra. As you
can see, I have lived on Tarra for
quite a long time. My focus has
transcended the matters that are to
do with this continent only.

She smiles warmly.

KOA

Tyra, it would be great to take some
of your wisdom with us.

TYRA

Life on this planet is comfortable,
orderly. Maybe too orderly. Time will
show that this comfort is insufficient
to secure the future of the planet.

My mother used to tell me what
her mother used to tell her ... that a
Golden Tablet will be discovered to
suggest a plan for salvation. Tarra will
sing its planetary song and shift to
joy. Be aware – there might be two
plans. Future is born from unity.

*The moment that Tyra mentions the Golden Tablet,
father and son immediately look at one another as
if trying to get assurance that they heard what they
thought they did.*

With her last words, Tyra is wrapped in a whitish mist and disappears.

Only when Tyra's words stopped, did Tibar and Koa turn their heads towards Tyra but their eyes now meet a misty cloud.

From that mist, unfamiliar sounds reach them, adding to their confusion.

They look down following the meowing sound. Three cats walk out of the misty cloud.

Huma happily flies down from Koa's shoulder and hovers above the cats.

Tibar is still confused yet is coming to terms with the situation.

Koa is excited, his eyes open wide in a sheer yet pleasant disbelief.

KOA

> Romy, Rocco, Rory! Am I dreaming
> again?

All three cats meow in response; Koa rushes to touch them, and hugs all of them with one big hug.

37. INT. SPACESHIP MANNA-373 – DAY

The old woman, Tyra, who disappears from Tarra, immediately appears in the MANNA-373.

TYRA

> Captain Urros, what is my next
> assignment?

CAPTAIN URROS

Oh, yes. There is one already waiting for you.

TYRA

I look forward to it. By the way, how are they progressing on Tarra?

CAPTAIN URROS

I would say: average. Faro, for how much longer will the Tablet be effective?

FARO

6 HOURS in our time, 6 DAYS in their time. Captain, may I ask whether the Tarran people are aware of this count-down?

CAPTAIN URROS

No. They are not aware of the deadline.

FARO

Then, what are their chances of success? Where could they find guidance?

CAPTAIN URROS

Success is always one of the options, in every challenge. LIFE itself is a master guide. Those able to step deeper into the fabric of life are able to recognise the right guidance and find solutions. That is why they are presented with the Golden Tablet.

FARO

Why is Tarra facing a planetary critical event?

CAPTAIN URROS

Those events, the catastrophic events, are potentiality formed by the consciousness of the planet – though some might be caused by natural phenomena or influence of hostile civilisations.

The good news is that it is possible to calculate the time of catastrophic events. We follow the consciousness' progress in the dimension of evolution. Then, we schedule our supervision based on the guidance received from the specialists in the field.

FARO

Who are those specialists?

CAPTAIN URROS

They are the Lords of Timing. They give us estimated dates of maximum convergence of negative factors, which a civilization cannot survive should it continue in the same direction.

The planetary Tablets are continuously monitored. Close to the critical event, they are brought near the soil's surface to be discovered in time. From then on – enough clues are available to provide guidance towards salvation.

FARO

How can an event of immense significance for an entire planet, depend so much on the intuition of people?

CAPTAIN URROS

How else? Inhabitants on the planet need to learn to COOPERATE WITH LIFE on a subtle energy level.

All appearances are but mere embodiments of vibrations and frequencies – an ongoing video story, played out by the PRESENCE OF THE INVISIBLE.

Living beings progress as they learn to discern the energy pallet of everything they encounter. We can only help to some extent – as the Universal Laws command.

FARO

(appears to be listening long after the Captain finished his explanation)

Thank you, Captain.

38. INT. SPACESHIP MANNA-373 – DAY

As he leaves Faro, Captain Urros walks through a corridor within MANNA-373.

He greets several staff members on his way. One of these is Miss MARRY.

CAPTAIN URROS

Here is our "Academy on Board" teacher! Hi Miss Marry! Everything OK?

MISS MARRY

Oh, yes. Thank you. I understand, Faro has joined you recently. How is he doing?

CAPTAIN URROS

To connect theoretical knowledge with real events takes time. He will get there. He is not the first cadet on this ship. You started that way too, Miss Marry.

MISS MARRY

I remember. At certain moments, it felt like all knowledge disappeared, or if not – it did not seem useful. It is an interesting process. I am glad it is behind me.

She pauses until she files the memories back.

MISS MARRY (CONT'D)

I hope, Captain, you will visit our Academy soon. Our cadets have not

seen you there for quite some time.
You are the epitome of their dreams.

CAPTAIN URROS

I am planning to!

Miss Marry bids farewell to Captain Urros with the signature body language GREETING of the MANNA-373.

39. EXT. CONTINENT 1, STREET – DAY

Surrounded by the three cats, Tibar and Koa (with Huma) walk away from the scene with the old woman.

TIBAR

I wonder how real that old woman
who disappeared was? In any case,
her words deeply resonated with me.

KOA

Huma obviously liked her vibes!

TIBAR

(pointing to the cats)

Look, these three cats are like
replicas of the cats you met in your
dream?

KOA

Maybe, they are not just replicas.
Maybe they are the originals!

Koa smiles and runs towards a beautiful reddish park they can see nearby.

The cats immediately start running behind him.

Huma follows, occasionally checking on each cat.

Tibar follows them at his own pace.

40.   EXT. CONTINENT 1, PARK – DAY

In the park, Koa plays with the cats on the grass.

Purplish Huma is perched at the ruddy tree, from where he can see Tibar as well.

41.   EXT. CONTINENT 1, PARK – DAY

Tibar arrives to the park following Koa and the animals.

As he steps into the park, three Milo operatives approach him.

They wear unusual caps and their standard grey clothes that resemble uniforms.

OPERATIVE 1

Nice day!

TIBAR

Yes, it is. Great to be outside.

OPERATIVE 1

Are you from this area?

TIBAR

Not really. How about you?

OPERATIVE 2

We are from a very different place.

TIBAR

What do you mean?

OPERATIVE 1

You are so unusual in your purple
robes on this red continent. You must
be from a different continent.

*Tibar notices that his question was not answered.
Not rushing to continue this conversation, he makes a
significant pause.*

TIBAR

I am actually a very ordinary citizen
but, yes, I have in mind a special
project for which it would be good to
have more people involved.

*The three operatives gradually reposition themselves
to stand at the corners of an invisible equilateral
triangle.*

*We SEE them generate a triangular field of MENTAL
ENERGY. Tibar is unaware of this.*

OPERATIVE 1

Sounds great. We would be very
interested to hear about it.

TIBAR

I think, Tarra is nearing a difficult
time and needs help...

As Tibar utters this sentence, he starts to feel progressively weaker.

Huma picks up on this development, utters a very high pitched sound and swiftly flies to Tibar.

Tibar collapses. The three men instantly leave.

After hearing Huma, Koa rushes to help his father.

The cats join him immediately.

All are helplessly gathered around Tibar's motionless body lying on the ground.

42. EXT. CONTINENT 1, PARK – DAY

A woman dressed in subtle red clothes (DORA, mid 40's, a calm listener that takes everything in) walks through the park.

As she notices a "purple" man (Tibar) laying on the reddish grass, Dora immediately joins the unusual group surrounding him.

DORA

> Hi, I am DORA. I hope you do not
> mind me approaching you? Do you
> need help?

KOA

> Yes, PLEASE! This is my father Tibar.
> I do not understand what has
> happened.

Dora swiftly starts examining Tibar's body then she performs certain circular movements above it.

After a short while, Tibar opens his eyes.

He sees an unknown female face.

Koa is outside of his view.

TIBAR

Where is Koa, is everything alright
with him?

Koa moves for Tibar to see him.

KOA

Yes, it is. How are you, father?

TIBAR

I am fine. I AM FINE now.

DORA

Hi, Tibar, I am Dora. I was passing by
and noticed you lying on the ground
so I came to try to help.

TIBAR

Thank you. It is very kind of you.

KOA

Dora, your help is much appreciated.
Thank you so much!

DORA

If you would allow it, I think I have
little more work to do on you, Tibar?
You need to be able to stand and
walk.

TIBAR

Please, do.

Dora continues with the healing procedure. She repeats the circular movements over Tibar's head and legs.

Shortly after, Tibar stands up, but is still noticeably weakened.

TIBAR (CONT'D)

Excellent! What a pleasure just to be able to stand!

With Koa and Dora at his sides, Tibar takes some steps that lead them to a table and chairs in the park.

The animals follow, and all sit together around the table.

DORA

Tibar, do you feel stable now?

TIBAR

Yes, and no.

DORA

You need to rest for some time and all will be fine. Do you mind me asking where you are from?

TIBAR

We are from Continent 7.

DORA

How did you manage to enter our continent?

TIBAR

It was not a problem at all. We simply flew in.

DORA

Odd! It means the continental
magnetic curtains are not doing
their job anymore, and we will soon
experience intercontinental traffic —
which has never happened! By the
way, what made you come to our
continent, if I may ask?

*Noticing that Tibar's focus is unstable, Koa starts
answering.*

Tibar is quiet, economical with his energy.

KOA

My father and I are working on a
project, a planetary project, and it
is interesting that the continental
curtains are melting down at the
same time.

DORA

Sounds more than intriguing! How
about if we move to my house, which
is just around the corner, and give
Tibar more time to fully recover?

KOA

Father, what do you think?

TIBAR

Sorry, what did you say, Koa?

KOA

Dora is inviting us to her place!

                    TIBAR

     I see.

He looks at Dora.

                TIBAR (CONT'D)

     As long as our menagerie will not
     disturb you, I do not mind. Thank
     you.

                    DORA

     You are all welcome then. Be my
     guests!

This kind offer cheers everyone, even Dora.

43.   EXT. CONTINENT 1, DORA'S GARDEN – DAY

*We see Tibar, Dora and Koa, with Huma and three cats,
reaching the street entrance to Dora's garden.*

Dora effortlessly enters the garden.

*Next, we watch Tibar at the garden gate undergoing a
scanning procedure.*

After a few seconds:

                MACHINE VOICE

     Permission requested!

                    DORA

     Permanent permission given.

*Each guest is being scanned and approved before they
step through the garden gate.*

44.   INT. CONTINENT 1, DORA'S HOUSE – DAY

The interior of Dora's house is dominated by pale RED colours.

In a living space flooded with light and abundant with house plants, Dora plays the harp. This pleasant interior effortlessly merges with the garden.

Relaxed, Tibar rests on an armchair.

45.   EXT. CONTINENT 1, DORA'S GARDEN – DAY

The tranquil sounds of a harp are in the air.

Dora and Tibar slowly walk through the garden. They occasionally stop by some plants and observe them.

We do not hear their conversation, yet their body language reveals a harmonious and considerate interaction.

It is getting dark.

> TIBAR
>
> It was a great day, Dora. Thanks for your kind hospitality.

> DORA
>
> My pleasure. How do you feel, Tibar?

> TIBAR
>
> I feel almost fully recovered.

He stops for a while, as if still deciding whether to say what is in his mind.

Dora is patiently attentive.

TIBAR (CONT'D)

I was thinking that it will be
better if we move on, and stop
inconveniencing you. We should
perhaps leave tomorrow, if that is
fine with you.

Tibar is certain that he wants to pursue his mission without digressions, yet he would not like to leave Dora without telling her about the Tablet. She helps him by opening an opportunity for it.

DORA

Before you leave, can we go for a
walk to my favourite forest? I would
like you to see it in the early morning.

TIBAR

Sure. If it is not too far to walk.

DORA

We will fly there, and then walk only
as long as it is comfortable to you.

TIBAR

Sounds ideal.

46.   EXT. ABOVE CONTINENT 1 – EARLY MORNING

A misty morning, with reddish hues in the air.

Closer to the ground, the hexagonal fractality appears everywhere: in urban planning as well as in the landscaping of forests, water features and meadows. From high above, the configuration of Continent 1 is still vague.

Several pyramobiles fly in different directions, and one of them is Dora's pyramobile.

She can be seen through the window.

47.   EXT. CONTINENT 1, GREAT FOREST – EARLY MORNING

A jungle-like red forest immersed in morning freshness.

Butterflies still asleep on flowery bushes. Rare birds sing.

Dora and Tibar follow the neatly meandering pedestrian pathways.

Ponds and cascading canals break through the dense body of forest.

She is calm yet cheerful. He is in his mind.

Dora stops, so does he.

Dora looks in Tibar's eyes, warmly.

He manages to sustain that sudden visit of her Soul.

DORA

Tibar, I feel something big is always on your mind and is bothering you. If I could be of any help, please share it. BESIDES, I would like to hear more about the reasons for your visit to this continent.

TIBAR

You are right, there is something big that puzzles me. I consider it immensely important, yet I am not

sure how you will receive it – hence
I have been quiet about it. Dora, I
would like to stay your friend, but I
worry whether you will consider me
a lunatic after I disclosed to you what
occupies my mind.

DORA

Tibar, I cannot reject somebody just
because they are grappling with a big
puzzle. Relax and let your words flow.

TIBAR

I was digging in my garden...

Tibar's voice fades away.

*We see the couple following the scenic pathways
through the forest, yet we do not hear Tibar telling the
rest of the story.*

After a while:

TIBAR (CONT'D)

Does this make sense to you?

DORA

Perfectly. I did not know about
the Golden Tablet, yet I have been
sensing for some time that the
lifestyle on Tarra has reached a peak
of some kind, and that this perpetual
sameness is wearing ourselves down.
Once the decline begins, something
has to stop it before it is too late.

I am with you. I think that however
puzzling the signs given by the Tablet

are, they point to a certain direction.
So, it is already a great help.

Thanks for opening yourself, Tibar.
You might not be aware, but you
have helped me just by sharing your
truth.

*Deep silence from both parties. Satisfaction in the air,
as if a great reconciliation has been reached.*

TIBAR

I think, you need to see the Tablet!

48.   EXT. CONTINENT 1, DORA'S GARDEN – DAY

*Tibar and Dora sit in Dora's garden flooded by red
foliage.*

*Tibar is showing her the hand-copied content of the
Golden Tablet.*

Dora holds the Golden Tablet in her hands.

DORA

I feel an enhanced mental clarity and
a distinctive inner-warmth.

*With both of her palms on the Tablet and eyes closed,
as if downloading a vision, she recites:*

DORA (CONT'D)

IN THE TIME OF GREAT DANGER, THE
SONG OF TARRA COMES FROM ALL –
AS ONE.

*Still absorbing its energy, Dora hands the Golden Tablet
to Tibar and takes from him its paper copy. She reads:*

DORA (CONT'D)

"... Tarra should vibrate in unison..."
Perhaps, "VIBRATE IN UNISON" is the
resonance of the singing voices?

TIBAR

I was thinking exactly the same thing.
Sound is a primordial power, and
collective singing can utilise it. Dora,
it feels so good to meet a like-minded
Soul!

DORA

I wish I could help more. I sense the
power of the Golden Tablet and the
immensity of its enigmatic message.
Now I understand why you cannot
stop thinking about it.

No wonder you are preoccupied
with finding a way to translate this
abstract guidance into concrete
action.

TIBAR

Thank you, Dora. Your words are
reinforcing my determination.

DORA

I am GLAD they do.

They exchange warm and supportive mutual glances.

TIBAR

I believe there is a way to succeed
in this challenge. I am also aware

that such achievement transcends my personal power. That points me towards a collective action – even though nothing has ever been done through a group effort of the Tarran people.

DORA

But it does not mean that it will never be done. WE CAN DO THAT.

TIBAR

(repeats mechanically)

Yes. WE CAN DO THAT.

Tibar stops and listens to what he has just said; actually, what Dora said.

TIBAR (CONT'D)

Am I hearing you correctly? Does the "WE" include YOU?

DORA

Yes. That is exactly what I meant!

TIBAR

Does it also mean we do not have to rush to leave your house?

DORA

Of course not.

They smile.

DORA (CONT'D)

By the way, Tibar, those five lines on
the Tablet, could they be a musical
stave and the small triangles on them
– musical notes?

49. INT. CONTINENT 1, DORA'S HOUSE – EARLY
     EVENING

*Dora and Tibar are in her living room. Their chat is out
of earshot.*

*Koa enters the living room. Huma and the three cats
follow.*

KOA

Hi, I thought you are still outside?

TIBAR

We had an early start, so are already
back from the beautiful forest.

KOA

How was it?

DORA

I hope Tibar managed to enjoy it.

Koa is surprised with Dora's words and slightly worried.

KOA

Is everything OK with you, father?

                        TIBAR

    Yes, yes it is. I was too much in
    my thoughts, as I am still trying to
    figure out how to proceed with the
    guidance of the Tablet. Dora picked
    up on my worries, and we talked
    about the Tablet. She has decided to
    join us.

                        KOA

    That is fantastic. It is THREE of us
    now – I like that number! We will
    have a bigger probability to disagree!

*He says this cheekily while looking at Tibar and Dora
with a smile that disarms both of them.*

*The moment Koa utters those words, Huma starts
singing its cheerful tune.*

The three cats meow as if saying "do not forget us".

                    KOA (CONT'D)

    Have a nice evening.

Koa makes a move to leave. Cats and Huma follow him.

50.   EXT. CONTINENT 1 – EARLY EVENING

*Omnia flies across Continent 1, due South. It gets
darker outside as it flies.*

*We see less and less urban configurations below the
pyramobile.*

*The ground gradually becomes a dark carpet dotted
with twinkling lights.*

51.   INT. OMNIA, CONTINENT 1 – NIGHT

Koa is happy, piloting in the company of the three cats and Huma.

The cats are loafing on the floor, surrounding Huma.

KOA

(talking to himself, or, equally, to his animal friends)

Isn't it exciting to fly – even in a machine? The world looks so different when we change our observational point. You know that, Huma? Don't you?

HUMA

Know that.

As if to illustrate the statement, Huma makes several circles just below Omnia's ceiling, and lands on Koa's lap.

The cats move from the floor and join Huma.

As the cats pack themselves on Koa's lap, Huma pops up not to be suffocated and settles on Romy's back.

KOA

Ok. I love you all.

52.   EXT. CONTINENT 1, GREAT FOREST – NIGHT

76th parallel. Darkness all around.

Deep silence occasionally pierced by the odd sounds from nocturnal birds.

Koa sits at the tranquil interface of the two giants: the Great South Forest and the Polar Lake. He watches the starry sky and the horizon.

Huma is on his shoulder. The cats sit around attentively.

After a while, a UFO exits Tarra, being visible for just a few seconds after emerging from the inside of the planet.

Acting as if they have noticed the UFO, the cats immediately run towards it.

Soon, another UFO enters Tarra.

Koa is excited.

KOA

> Huma, look! Somebody flies between the celestial globes! I cannot even begin to imagine how sensational that must be? Would it not be great to meet those visitors of Tarra?

Koa looks around and notices that the cats are not back.

KOA (CONT'D)

> Huma, could you please call the cats.

Huma utters its signature sound.

Koa continues his observation.

KOA (CONT'D)

> For some reason, here on Tarra, we live isolated from other civilizations. How would we host visitors from other planets when we hardly host members of other houses at our

home!? WE are either not ready to
meet them yet or we will never be,
because such is Tarra's PROGRAMME.

*Romy, Rocco and Rory hurriedly emerge from behind
the bushes.*

KOA (CONT'D)

Good ones. Let us go back!

53.   EXT. CONTINENT 1, DORA'S GARDEN – DAY

Pleasant moments in the garden.

*Tibar and Dora stand by a flowery bush. They observe a
huge fuchsia pink butterfly with wings opened widely,
and compare it with a drawing in Dora's hands.*

Nearby, we see Koa playing with the cats.

Huma is perched on a tree branch.

DORA

Tibar, you seem to like geometry and
numbers!?

TIBAR

How could I not, when the
description of everything boils down
to them? Numbers actually parade
in front of us, disguised as various
forms and objects. Geometry makes
them visible.

*As Tibar continues, we watch the drawing in Dora's
hands that shows a geometric analysis of the butterfly's
body with open wings.*

The golden ratio, the number Phi (1.618...), frequently appears on measuring lines.

TIBAR (CONT'D)

What preserves each shape are
the proportions between its
components. If we change the value
of a single element only, it will
disturb the existing proportions and
alter the shape.

Tibar points to some measurement values.

TIBAR (CONT'D)

So, the value of even the tiniest
element is crucial in defining the
whole – be it a shape or an event.

Tibar stops talking for a moment. His tone shifts from excited reflection to calm logic.

TIBAR (CONT'D)

You are aware of all this. I am not
sure why I am saying it?

DORA

Yes, I am aware. But it is so nice to
listen to you talking and experience
your excitement.

Dora looks at Tibar and their eyes lock briefly. As if paying no attention to that, she continues on the subject.

DORA (CONT'D)

Regardless of how long I have been
studying NATURE, my fascination

with it does not lessen. I particularly
have in mind the GOLDEN
PROPORTION, which impregnates
the entire creation — not only on the
level of visible forms, but also on
the formation processes within the
universe and the invisible realms
of mind and emotions. The unique
relationship between the two uneven
parts and the whole they make,
regulated by the golden proportion,
is ALSO the FINEST EXPRESSION of
HARMONIOUS UNITY and BEAUTY.

No wonder we find the golden
number Phi embodied in the shape
of this butterfly and in the dispersion
of the colours along its wings!

TIBAR

How mathematical beauty is!

*They turn silent and soak in this fascinating truth they
deeply revere.*

*Their nearly meditative state is soon interrupted by
Koa, who gets up from the grass nearby.*

*With the cat Romy in his hand, and from some distance,
he addresses Dora and his father:*

KOA

I will stroll around the
neighbourhood for a while!

TIBAR

Dora and me might go to the lake!
See you later.

KOA

Have a good time.

Koa turns toward the bushes:

KOA (CONT'D)

Huma, we are moving!

HUMA

Moving!

The bird flies towards Koa.

54.   EXT. CONTINENT 1, STREET – DAY

Koa is on the street walking away from Dora's garden. Huma is on his shoulder and Romy in his arms.

Rocco and Rory follow.

After several steps, Koa is surrounded with an invisible energy whirlpool that lifts him up. We see him disappear together with Huma and Romy.

At the last moment, the two other cats jump into the vibrating beam and disappear with them.

55.   EXT. CONTINENT 1, LAKE – DAY

Tibar and Dora walk by a small local lake. The promenade is highlighted by the rows of tall red trees.

TIBAR

Dora, would you like to hear about
how Koa was born?

DORA

Sure, I would love to! Koa is an exceptional young man. It seems he lives in a bigger reality than the one on Tarra.

We watch some situations that Tibar describes, at which point Tibar's voice goes off screen.

It is left for the production team to decide which scenes to illustrate.

TIBAR

On my 21st birthday, I decided to treat myself by visiting my favourite point by the local lake. I sat on the promenade and communicated with the water.

A young woman, Vera, who was passing by, slipped and fell into the lake.

I jumped and brought her out of the water. She was bruised, distressed and embarrassed. Because she did not mention having family or a home, we came to my house.

On that very day, the Celestial Dissemination Unit (CDU) was to beam down my (celestial) female partner. Machines remotely detected the female presence (of the 21-year-old girl) in my house, and moved on to check the rest of the Tarran population.

Since I was consumed by the presence of the beautiful girl, I completely forgot that it was my birthday and that my life partner was to be delivered to me. However, it was not until the next day that I realised all that.

Interestingly, I remember, Vera was not wet from falling into the water, and she never mentioned where she came from. Whether I will ever learn the secret behind her appearance – I don't know. It was either a genuine or a deliberate glitch of the Celestial Dissemination Unit on that day.

Regardless, I just prayed that a similar glitch will not remove Vera from my life.

At this instant, an irresistible tune from the tiny bird on the nearby tree starts to flood the space.

Dora and Tibar could not help but surrender to that frequency.

After some time in silence, they resume their conversation and continue walking.

TIBAR (CONT'D)

Fondness grew between me and Vera, and we decided to stay together. Vera was an exceptionally joyful woman, very much INTERESTED IN THE GEOMETRY OF SHAPES. Her hobby was to study the RELATIONSHIP BETWEEN FORMS AND THE ENERGY THEY EMIT.

She would observe this relationship through the frequency and the expression of that frequency across various mediums – sound, light, scent or movement. Hence, you could always find her surrounded by flowers, birds and butterflies.

As you are aware, every family on Tarra gets a 7-year old child from the CDU. However, Koa was CONCEIVED ON TARRA. He was born from a BIOLOGICAL mother on the last day of the year, the day G-49.

Vera moved on from this planet on Koa's 7th birthday.

She left lots of geometry drawings, sketches and paintings of flowers and butterflies. In her room we also found a peculiar BRACELET, which Koa placed on his left arm as soon as he could wear it comfortably.

DORA

I noticed it.

TIBAR

Vera used to spend so much time playing with Koa, walking in nature, watching the night sky, playing many musical instruments to him and laughing with him. She was also drawing butterflies and birds with him, and teaching him to communicate with them. All three of us used to play music together. Koa started to play the keyboard very young.

DORA

Koa has an unusual bird toy –
Huma?!

TIBAR

It is the toy his mother started to make for him. Koa was watching and listening to her explanations and visions very attentively. Since Vera left us, he has been keeping that unfinished toy by his bed for years. Then, he started to work on it and made Huma.

Have you noticed, he often speaks with Huma as if the bird is alive?

DORA

I think I have, but was not sure whether he speaks with himself or addresses Huma.

TIBAR

Most likely both.

DORA

Since Vera left, have you asked the Celestial Dissemination Unit (CDU) for another partner?

TIBAR

No.

56.   INT. MILO UNDERGROUND BASE – DAY

Transported to the Milo underground facility together with Koa and Huma, the three cats immediately turn invisible.

Moments later, Huma becomes invisible and stays constantly in Koa's vicinity.

57.   INT. MILO UNDERGROUND BASE – DAY

A technological room, full of various hi-tech equipment.

Koa is lying on a raised bed. One Milo operative is beside him.

A scanner runs over Koa's body. Results are followed on the screen. Scanning completed.

The invisible Huma is quiet the whole time, yet appears not idle.

KOA

Who are you?

MILO PERSON

As members of the Milo civilisation, we are the established guests of planet Tarra. We utilise the otherwise useless planet's interior.

KOA

May I ask why you are taking my body data?

MILO PERSON

We need your DNA and your body map for our archive, since we have not come across a being such as you. We noticed your presence at the 76th South parallel. No other residents of Tarra ever managed to exit their vehicles and walk in that energy intensive region. Obviously, it is not a problem for you.

KOA

I did not give you permission to take my DNA data!

MILO PERSON

True. We apologise, but our scientific enquiry is grand, and we cannot always afford to follow all Universal Laws.

Sometimes, to follow them would take more time than we are willing to waste on secondary issues and activities. You see, young man, we are very focused on enriching the galactic volume of knowledge with new discoveries.

KOA

Great focus, indeed. However, your approach is a violation of free will. According to the Universal Laws, it is forceful behaviour even though no extremely violent force is used. Crime and forcefulness can have

many forms. I request you delete all
information taken from me!

MILO PERSON

We will be very frank with you. As
mentioned, we do not follow the
Universal Ordinances to the letter,
and we defend it with the fact that
we are creative and want to expand
the variety of high quality living
beings, and their capacities. What is
wrong with that?

KOA

What makes you think that your
project, which is not in accord with
the Laws of the Universe, can be
seen as good?

MILO PERSON

Interesting perspective!

We will leave you to entertain
yourself with such thoughts, until you
find the answer for yourself.

KOA

I already have the answer: YOU
value YOUR ideas, your projects and
opinions more than the Universal
Laws.

It is because you still do not truly
understand what these Laws are and
what their true POWER is.

You have chosen to estrange yourself
from it, since it is an easier way to be,

and now you are justifying that step
by attributing magnificence to your
ideas and projects.

You completely misunderstand
freedom!

58.   INT. MILO UNDERGROUND BASE – DAY

*We follow the three invisible cats and observe their
INVISIBLE ENERGY in action.*

*Romy and Rory investigate the entire Underground
Base.*

*Rocco is in the same room as Koa, carefully observing
everything.*

*When Koa's biological data is taken, Rocco swiftly
erases it from the Milo's computers using its mental
energy.*

59.   INT. MILO UNDERGROUND BASE – DAY

KOA

Gentlemen, it was a pleasure
meeting you, and with your
permission I will greet you and
leave. I expect to be returned at the
location from which you took me.

MILO PERSON

Sure. The pleasure was ours. By the
way, we hope you will forget this
encounter with us. It would be useful

for you, otherwise – we will have to
meet again.

KOA

May I also ask you to return my bird
and three cats to me?

MILO PERSON

I am afraid, young man, we have not
noticed the creatures you are talking
about.

Koa is escorted outside the room.

MILO PERSON (CONT'D)

(instructs the remaining personnel)

As soon as this young man is back to
his people, keep an eye on him and
his family.

60.   EXT. CONTINENT 1, STREET – DAY (MOMENTS
      LATER)

*Out of thin air, Koa manifests at the exact location that
the Milo operatives beamed him from.*

Immediately after, the three cats and Huma manifest.

*As they all gather and enter Dora's garden, Koa stops
unexpectedly and puzzled sits on the grass.*

The cats and Huma spread around him.

KOA

(looking at Huma and each cat)

Wait a second, guys! I remember holding Romy in my hand, with Huma on my shoulder, and Rocco and Rory joining the transportation beam. So, ALL OF US WERE RELOCATED.

I also remember seeing you, dear cats, very briefly in the Milo's underground facility, in the instant we reached there. But then, you turned invisible. The same happened with Huma.

And look at you now! You are returning on your own – right!? The Milo people did not even see you there!

HOW could THEY then send you back, and WHY would they?

The cats listen, like kids caught doing forbidden things.

Huma flies off to a nearby flowery bush.

Koa addresses the cats:

KOA (CONT'D)

Sorry, my friends, I need to understand what is going on.

For some time, I was entertaining the thought of talking to you but was preoccupied with different things. However, now I would really appreciate if you talk to me.

The cats are silent and attentive.

KOA (CONT'D)

I see. Not only can you turn invisible!
You can also teleport yourselves!

The cats are still silent.

Koa collects them on his lap, and places them as to face him. He strokes them gently and continues in a loving voice:

KOA (CONT'D)

So, you are not really cats?

At that instant, Rory stretches towards Koa as if to emphasise that communication is taking place.

The following sentences that come from the cats, Koa hears clearly in his mind.

RORY CAT

Koa, you might say so.

KOA

Can you teach me teleportation?

Romy meows and adds:

ROMY CAT

We can try. If you are ready for it –
you will be able to do it.

Rocco changes position and focuses on Koa's face.

ROCCO CAT

We know you are.

KOA

Excellent! We'll do it tomorrow at
some suitable place.

61.   EXT. CONTINENT 1, MEADOW – DAY

*Koa, Huma and the three cats are on a meadow flooded
with a great variety of red flowers and butterflies.*

*Koa HOVERS around, at various heights, entertaining
his companions who run after him.*

After enough excitement, they all settle on the grass.

We follow their mental communication.

ROMY CAT

Your mind needs to be in harmony
with each of your cells. When you
connect the awareness of every cell
to your cerebral awareness – when
they all meet at one frequency, the
brain power projects that frequency
onto the location you want to move
to.

RORY CAT

If you cannot elevate the frequency
of every single cell to the frequency
level of the brain, bodily integrity
will not be preserved for the aimed
destination. The body will manifest
only partially.

What Romy and Rory explain, Rocco illustrates.

He disappears and reappears behind the short bushes about 30 meters away.

Then, with a "meow", he attracts Koa's and Huma's attention from afar.

Huma flies to meet Rocco, and then follows Rocco's walking back to the group.

ROMY CAT

We are only talking about teleportation within one planet. To teleport through the cosmic medium includes more variables.

ROCCO CAT

We can teleport objects – as we already did by bringing Huma back with us. We just project their exact frequency to the desired location and they will be there. It is easier than teleporting a living being, because all particles of an object already vibrate at one frequency – there is no cacophony between them.

ROMY CAT

Shall we teleport Huma to show you?

Koa moves Huma from his shoulder to the grass.

The three cats position themselves in an equilateral triangle surrounding Huma.

Soon, Huma disappears.

The three cats and Koa remain on the meadow.

62.   EXT. CONTINENT 1, DORA'S GARDEN – DAY

Tibar is sitting in the garden and browses through his diary. He stops at a certain page and thinks.

A butterfly lands on that page. We see the sentence: "I must, I want, I will succeed".

After a while, the butterfly takes off and dances away.

Tibar watches the butterfly disappear above a bush. At the same time, Huma lands on that very bush.

Tibar turns his head around expecting to see Koa. Surprised by witnessing his absence, he poses a question to the metal toy.

TIBAR

Hi, Huma! Where is Koa?

Huma flies to Tibar and lands on his shoulder.

Tibar takes it into his hands, and observes the colourful toy with the admiration of a child.

Huma starts one tune perfectly suitable to Tibar.

Tibar is comforted as if he has received a very concrete answer.

63.   EXT. CONTINENT 1, MEADOW – DAY

Koa stands still with both hands by his body.

Visually, we follow his mental focus on unifying his cellular vibrations and harmonising them with the vibrational coordinates of his brain.

As full resonance is reached, Koa dematerialises and disappears from the meadow.

By the power of his brain energy, his invisible light body is relocated instantly.

64. EXT. CONTINENT 1, DORA'S GARDEN – DAY
     (MOMENTS LATER)

Koa appears in Dora's garden, behind his father who still holds Huma in his hands.

Huma is singing. Koa walks forward so that his father can see him.

KOA

Hi, father. I see Huma is entertaining you.

TIBAR

It is such a cute toy. Even though it is a collection of mostly metal and electronic pieces, there seems to be more to it.

KOA

I think so.

Koa gets closer to his father, smiles and takes Huma from his father's palm.

KOA (CONT'D)

I am afraid, we will have to leave now. This was not really a planned visit.

Tibar responds with a typical parental unconditional acceptance.

TIBAR

It is fine, enjoy yourself.

Koa, with Huma on his hand, walks towards the garden exit.

65. EXT. CONTINENT 1, STREET – DAY (CONTINUOUS)

Koa walks for a while with Huma on his hand.

KOA

Well done, Huma! You are doing great!

HUMA

Doing great.

After saying that, Huma starts singing.

Koa sits on a bench and places Huma next to him.

Soon, Huma's tune stops abruptly as the bird disappears from the bench.

Seconds later, Koa disappears.

66. EXT. CONTINENT 1, MEADOW – DAY (MOMENTS LATER)

Aerial view of the meadow.

Motionless, the three cats still hold a triangular formation. They face the central point of a virtual triangle.

Soon, Huma appears in that virtual triangle. Seconds later, Koa manifests but outside the cats' triangle.

Koa and the cats jump in excitement.

Huma flies around showing some pirouettes not seen before.

67.   EXT. COSMIC VASTNESS

We see a smaller spaceship (TRAVIS) flying through space.

It features a logo that belongs to the owners of the Diffusion Centre on Tarra's North Pole.

68.   INT. SPACESHIP TRAVIS – DAY

The TRAVIS crew comprises of two MALES and one FEMALE.

FEMALE

So many daily reports have been
missing from Tarra recently.

MALE 1

IT IS unprecedented in Tarra's history.
What could possibly interfere with
their legendary diligence?

MALE 2

Hopefully, we'll discover it soon. We
are very close to Tarra.

The first signs of Tarra's continents are visible on the computer screen.

MALE 2 (CONT'D)

I am detecting no magnetic curtains
around the Tarra's continents! Air
traffic is unusually busy.

Invisible to Tarra population's frequency range, the
TRAVIS spaceship is descending further.

MALE 1

Look, SO MANY people are mingling
around, outside their houses!

All of the crew are visibly surprised.

FEMALE

Something unusual is going on here.

69.   EXT. SPACESHIP TRAVIS – DAY

The TRAVIS spaceship flies over the Great North Forest,
then over the Polar Lake towards the North Pole.

The Diffusion Centre is becoming visible.

The spaceship lands vertically, 100% in the centre of
the roof.

70.   INT. SPACESHIP TRAVIS – DAY

The opening of the hexagonal door in the craft's floor is
activated. As the floor opens, we see a hexagon deeply
embossed on the building's roof.

Another command opens that hexagonal roof section,
allowing the stairs from the craft to stretch to the floor
inside the building.

With the roof's opening, the lights inside the building turn on. We see the first crew member starting to go down the stairs.

71. INT. DIFFUSION CENTRE – DAY

Through the opening in the roof, using the unfolded stairs, the crew descends directly to the central space of the building.

They see a deserted battlefield, the six robots in pieces scattered around, and a hole in the external wall.

Shocked, they rush into the computer room. The equipment there is still working.

They sit down to check the specifics.

After a while, having analysed some data:

MALE 1

The planetary frequency algorithm
has been changed!

FEMALE

And a new programme installed to
cause a frequency decrease!

A thoughtful pause followed by a eureka moment.

As if recalling a similar experience with the Milo people, she exclaims in full conviction:

FEMALE (CONT'D)

Milo!

And immediately spills out a solution:

FEMALE (CONT'D)

Let us restore the algorithm and call
the Milo to a Galactic Tribunal.

72.   INT. GALACTIC TRIBUNAL – DAY

*At the gathering of the Galactic Tribunal, the Milo's
representative and the Tarra's Diffusion Centre
representative fight for their interests.*

*The DC representative is the female member of the
TRAVIS crew.*

MILO REP

(addresses the DC representative)

Our project Mélange is beneficial
even to you, since we believe that we
can produce a human with a capacity
far bigger than the capacity of the
workforce you have on Tarra now. So,
in the long term, we will all benefit.

As you know, if a civilization fails to
advance, it will stagnate. Despite
all the risks, Milo's always prefer
progress rather than stagnation.

DC REP

We have already invested a lot into
developing the research centre
on Tarra, where people live most
comfortably – relaxed and fully
focused on daily tasks.

Why don't you seek another location
for your project Mélange?

MILO REP

We have, but are still waiting for the
answer from the Galactic Assembly.
Since we believe our project is urgent
and on our end all is ready for it,
we see no reason to prolong its
beginning.

DC REP

Without the agreement of the
wide celestial community, you
give yourself freedom to work on
destroying Tarra's population! You
have penetrated our facilities and
changed the frequency adjustment
parameters to suit your needs. As
a consequence, we see an utter
disorientation of the population of
Tarra. They are unable to focus and
do their daily work.

*With great anticipation, both representatives look at
the judge.*

JUDGE

Thank you, esteemed
representatives. Tarra is a precious
asset in the field of galactic research
and should remain so.

He turns to the Milo representative.

JUDGE (CONT'D)

Milo, you are asked to cease all your
activities related to reducing the
planetary frequency of Tarra.

73. INT. MILO UNDERGROUND BASE – DAY

Among other personnel, we see the Milo representative from the Galactic Tribunal.

MILO PERSON

What is the verdict?

MILO REP

Our ancestors are known as men of courage, who would not give in when faced with challenges. Honouring them means fighting for OUR visions. Let us finish this Tarra episode in a few days.

Decisively, he gives an order to the technical personnel.

MILO REP (CONT'D)

We should work directly on the crystalline grid. Focus on it, and make sure its frequency is decreasing VERY QUICKLY.

74. INT. SPACESHIP MANNA-373 – DAY

Miss Marry, the teacher in "Academy on Board", passes Faro seated by his desk.

MISS MARRY

Hi, Faro! Here you are.

FARO

Miss Marry, how nice to see you outside the teaching theatre.

MISS MARRY

How are you doing in the shoes of a
crewman?

FARO

Learning every second. The Academy
was just an introduction to real life.
I am following an interesting planet
called Tarra.

MISS MARRY

Bear in mind what we were saying in
the classroom: "Do not buy into the
drama of events, which some planets
are experiencing in order to move
on in their evolution. Do not judge
anybody's evolution level. Instead --

FARO / MISS MARRY

(as one voice)

--BE COMPASSIONATE, and ACCEPT
them as they are."

Both laugh.

Miss Marry moves on.

*Faro presses the button marked "planets / Tarra" to
watch the latest video update.*

WE WATCH:

*Pyramobiles fly everywhere, within the continents and
across the continents.*

*An unusually large number of people are outside
their homes. Many are in nature, many on the streets
chatting with passers-by.*

Some still try to work on their research, then quickly give up and go outside.

As we watch the above:

MALE NARRATOR (V.O.)

The frequency on Tarra is
progressively decreasing.
Consequently, the energy curtains
around the continents have melted
away and the magnetic fields of the
continents are starting to merge.
This influx of different energy is
an additional challenge to people.
They do not feel well, but utterly
confused and lost on their planet.
Social disorder is swiftly engulfing
all continents. A solution to this
unprecedented situation is the most
needed thing on the planet.

Faro presses the button "Tarra" to stop the video.

He looks around and is relieved by noticing Miss Marry return, then walks to meet her.

FARO

Miss Marry! Do you have a moment?
Can I please ask you something?

MISS MARRY

Sure.

FARO

Are you familiar with Tarra's current
state of affairs?

MISS MARRY

To some extent.

FARO

Would we ever know the reasons for the weakening of Tarra's frequency?

MISS MARRY

Even if we know, the permission to reverse that course does not sit with us.

FARO

But, what if things get far too dangerous for the Tarran people?

MISS MARRY

We do not fly around the galaxy with a magic wand and spare civilizations from suffering or even extinction. The Universal Laws are clear on that topic.

FARO

What is clear about such situations?

MISS MARRY

Those situations pertain to evolution and evolution requires effort from the subjects in question. I might remind you on how we define "efforts".

FARO

Please.

MISS MARRY

Effort means the CAPACITY to
GENERATE ENERGY necessary
to COMBAT ENTROPY. For life to
continue, generated energy has to be
used to PREVENT DECAY and create
an ORDER instead. This is a natural
canon. How much will one individual
or civilisation struggle, to maintain
in order and stay in existence, varies.
However, it does not mean that
carelessness rules life.

FARO

Are you talking about the Universal
Laws of Equilibrium?

MISS MARRY

VERY GOOD, Faro!

*Miss Marry leaves Faro yet after a few steps she walks
back to address him.*

MISS MARRY (CONT'D)

By the way, for how long more will
the POWER of the Golden Tablet will
be available to Tarra?

FARO

Three days in their time – about
3 hours for us. Miss Marry, I am
so anxious not knowing the final
outcome.

MISS MARRY

Anxiety can strengthen your spiritual
muscles – if you withstand the
challenge. It gives you an opportunity
to acquire a fresh and positive
perspective, which is very precious.

FARO

I will do my best, Miss Marry. You
have never stopped teaching me.

75.   EXT. CONTINENT 1, DORA'S HOUSE – DAY

*Tibar, Dora and Koa sit comfortably in Dora's high
BALCONY with a beautiful view to her lavish garden.*

*The three cats laze around. Huma is quiet, yet
occasionally flies from one cat to another.*

There is a tension-free thoughtful atmosphere.

KOA

Father, I think we cannot wait
anymore...

The planet seems to be heading
towards more difficulties and
towards an utter dysfunctionality.
According to my understanding and
knowledge, what can stabilise the
field are CORRECT FREQUENCIES.

TIBAR

I see. But how could we know which
frequency is needed?

I know the vibrational sound
frequency of tulips and some other
flowers, but not more than that.

KOA

I have to share something with
you. As the energy curtains around
the continents have started to
melt, I used that opportunity to
visit every continent on Tarra.
Since I am interested in vibrations
and frequencies, I measured the
frequency of each continent.

Then, I figured out that the frequency
of each continent corresponds to
one of seven musical notes. The
only exception is Continent 5,
associated with the 5th major energy
point of the planet that stands for
communication, relationships and
self-expression. This fact could
explain why the citizens of Tarra have
no affinity to communicate with
others outside their family.

Why this frequency is not in balance,
WHAT, or perhaps WHO, disbalanced
it – is another topic.

DORA

It seems that Continent 5, therefore
the planet as a whole, is craving
a particular frequency. Why don't
we provide it through a global
solfeggio ceremony? Solfeggio sound
harmonies will synchronise the
CONTINENTAL and GLOBAL fields,

and escort Tarra out of the current chaos.

Tarra will also align with the tones and rhythms that underpin the entire universe.

KOA

Exactly. Tarra can and will attune, heal and ascend!

TIBAR

Is it possible that all this globally growing chaos is the result of a frequency misalignment of a single continent?

KOA

There is more to it! When I designed Huma, my intention was not just to have a colourful toy around me all the time. I designed it as a frequency-detecting and recording apparatus.

From analysing the data that Huma was collecting from our global flights, I also noticed that the overall frequency of the planetary magnetic field has started to decline – just around the time, father, when you discovered the Golden Tablet.

I was therefore not surprised when energy curtains between the continents started to disappear or with the planetary disorientation that followed. Interestingly, I could not attribute this odd change to any outside factor.

This is because, as we are aware, Tarra's sky is sealed from certain celestial influences in order to secure the stability of life on it. So, if the cause does not come from outside the planet, then it must come from the planet.

TIBAR

How do you mean that?

KOA

I did not need to wait too long, to find out that it must be the case. Father, forgive me for not sharing all this earlier. Only now, can I put the pieces together.

TIBAR

No worries. I always trust you, and believe you would tell me if anything is worth sharing.

KOA

Your support is so crucial for my confidence to explore. Thank you, father.

Koa gets up, goes to his father and hugs him while Tibar remains seated.

KOA (CONT'D)

From the time of flying our pyramobile on my own, I noticed

UFOs going in and out of Tarra's
South Pole region.

It was not a one off, but a regular
activity. My suspicion is that
an underground civilization is
performing either some experiments
which accidentally affect us on the
surface, or – perhaps – deliberately.

TIBAR

We are obviously in a dire situation.
Have you thought in more detail
about the global solfeggio ceremony?

KOA

I have, and that includes a very
practical application of the Golden
Tablet, and its 6 detachable triangles,
by people that will sing solfeggios.

So, we must have a representative
from each continent to complete a
planetary circle of those singers.

With Dora from Continent 1, you,
father, from Continent 7, we would
need five more people – one each
from the remaining five continents.
By the correct tuning frequencies and
the power of the Golden Tablet set,
harmonization will take place and
Tarra will transcend this disgraceful
state.

We will all recognise that moment.
A wave of smiles and joy will travel
around the planet to include, revive

and upgrade every single resident on
it.

TIBAR

Sounds great! But how do we
proceed now? How can we identify
those five people?

DORA

Maybe, their mission is to find us?

All smile.

TIBAR

Would we be able to generate
enough power to shift and harmonise
the entire planet just by singing?

KOA

Each of the seven people will stand
in the middle of the open Pyramid at
the Central Square of their continent.
These Pyramids are rooted into the
crystalline grid of the planet.

As such, they will send the solfeggio
frequencies, amplified by the Tablet
and its triangles, directly to the
energy skeleton of Tarra.

If we could see the entire frequency
injection into Tarra's body, it would
be a spectacular display of sounds
and colours circulating through its
structural pathways. Yes, enough
power will be generated!

Singing the solfeggios will last 49 minutes, and Tarra will heal and rejuvenate.

Father, you have always believed in the Golden Tablet!? It is now time to witness the truth about it.

TIBAR

It is time, Koa. I unshakably believe in the Tablet, and I wish to add something.

According to my daily monitoring, it appears that every 7 days, the Golden Tablet shows its content. However, the intensity of the purple colour, that conjures up that content, changes during the month and is strongest on the very last day of the month – the 49th day.

This makes me believe that the strongest influence of the energy from the Dimension, which communicates with Tarra via this Golden Tablet, is on the last day of the month.

DORA

We should then perform the solfeggio ceremony on the last day of this month, which is coincidently the last day of the year too!

TIBAR

Yes. That way, we will capitalise on the guidance and help that we are

obviously receiving from somewhere.
What a blessing!

KOA

After all, the Tablet seems
to be a high-dimensional
technology bestowed on Tarra; a
multidimensional device – not just a
piece of shiny material.

DORA

So, we all agree to schedule our
Solfeggio ceremony for G-49.

But, Tibar, is that not Koa's birthday?
And it is in two days!

TIBAR

Is it? Already!? Then, I want to
celebrate Koa's birthday in a new era
of the planet!

76.   INT. CONTINENT 1, DORA'S HOUSE – DAY

Koa designs the casings for the Golden Triangles and the Tablet.

We see numerous sketches. All show a looped cord attached to the casing, which turns the Triangle and the Tablet into pendants of a simple necklace.

Tibar and Dora are with Koa discussing the sketches.

77.   INT. CONTINENT 1, DORA'S HOUSE – DAY

Tibar, Dora and Koa are around a worktop with all their handcraft lined up on it.

The three cats are together on the floor.

> ### TIBAR
>
> Well done everyone! Koa, which continents would you like to work on?

> ### KOA
>
> I would be happy to work on Continents 4, 5 and 6, in which case you two go to Continents 2 and 3.
>
> I assume I will use Omnia and you will fly in Dora's pyramobile?

> ### DORA
>
> Yes. That is fine.

> ### KOA
>
> What about the cats? Do you want one with you?

> ### DORA
>
> Oh, yes, please! How about Rocco?

> ### KOA
>
> Is that ok with you, Rocco?

Sleepy Rocco opens one of his eyes, then meows.

Everybody is pleased with Rocco's response.

THE THIRD PART

78.   EXT. CONTINENT 4, STREET – DAY

Koa is with Huma, Rory and Romy, on Continent 4 in the midst of an unusually busy urban environment.

This continent is dominated by colour green. Inside parks and forests it is difficult to distinguish people since they wear green clothes.

Koa approaches "green" people intending to find somebody interested in what he has to offer. Some people stop and talk, some do not.

> KOA
>
> Would you like to help people and the planet?

> PERSON 1
>
> Yes. I would. But I do not see how.

> KOA
>
> What if somebody else sees? Would you not want to try?

> PERSON 1
>
> I have no reason to believe them.

79.   EXT. CONTINENT 4, STREET – DAY

A view on a crowded open space.

Movements in all directions, indistinguishable noise.

Koa tries to engage passers-by. We see his action from the distance and hear the following selection of futile dialogues.

WOMAN (O.S.)

Interesting idea. How do you know it will work?

KOA (O.S.)

I know it will.

WOMAN (O.S.)

How can you know?

KOA (O.S.)

Do you have a child?

WOMAN (O.S.)

Yes, I have a girl. Why do you ask?

KOA (O.S.)

Do you love your child?

WOMAN (O.S.)

What a question! Of course I do.

KOA (O.S.)

How do you know you love her?

People are passing by Koa. The crowd's noise does not change.

OLDER MAN (O.S.)

I am sorry, I cannot commit to something too vague.

                          KOA (O.S.)

              It might be too vague to your mind.
              But what about your heart?

*We still watch the fluid and noisy crowd while following
Koa's conversation.*

                       WOMAN 2 (O.S.)

              I was thinking about a solution to this
              growing disorientation.

                          KOA (O.S.)

              That is great! Can you see what is
              written on this paper?

                       WOMAN 2 (O.S.)

              This paper? It is empty! What makes
              you think something is on it? Are
              you trying to trick people using their
              vulnerability during these difficult
              circumstances?

                          KOA (O.S.)

              Sorry for inspiring your thoughts in
              such a direction.

*With his animal friends, Koa is now heading towards
the Central Square with the massive open Pyramid.*

80.   EXT. CONTINENT 2, STREET – DAY

*Tibar and Dora stand a few metres apart in the crowd
of the orangey continent, attempting to make people
interested in Tarra's salvation ceremony.*

Dora holds Rocco in her hands.

We observe many of their encounters with the passers-by and witness some from a close distance.

TIBAR

There is a way to help Tarra. Do you want to know more about it?

MAN 1

Yes. Why not!?

We do not hear Tibar's explanation. After a while:

MAN 1 (CONT'D)

I see. It sounds like an excellent fantasy to me. Good luck!

81.   EXT. CONTINENT 2, STREET – DAY

Rocco, in Dora's hands, attracts attention.

YOUNG MAN

What is that cute black creature?

DORA

A voyager from another planet.

YOUNG MAN

And is still here, despite this chaos?

DORA

Or, maybe, just because of this chaos?

They both smile. The young man moves on.

Shortly afterwards, Dora is in another conversation.

DORA (CONT'D)

It is time to get together and think
about the solution for this planet.

WOMAN

Exactly! Do you know somebody
eager to do that?

DORA

Yes. It is me.

WOMAN

I am afraid, I do not feel good. It
has been like that for some time.
Actually, I am useless.

82.   EXT. CONTINENT 2, STREET – DAY

Tibar walks a few steps to join Dora and Rocco.

TIBAR

Dora, I thought people on Tarra,
how would I say it, were not that
much different or opinionated at
least when it comes to a matter
so essential as the salvation of the
planet.

DORA

In normal times, we were more
reasonable, I believe. This situation
is different and scary. It is easy to
understand those attitudes. People
are not themselves.

TIBAR

You are right. Still, in this big crowd,
there must be a soul that resonates
with us.

DORA

Let us sit and relax for a while!

83.   EXT. CONTINENT 4, CENTRAL SQUARE – DAY

*Koa, Huma and the two cats arrive at the greenish
Central Square.*

*Koa wears his necklace with the visible pendant – the
Golden Triangle.*

*A young man, FABIO (early 30s, quick mind behind
a curious face), dressed in distinctive green robes,
approaches Koa.*

FABIO

Something has attracted me to you,
so much so that I had to come and
say hello. My name is Fabio.

KOA

Hi, Fabio. I am Koa. Thanks for
coming.

Interestingly, I have something to
share with you that might give a
fuller meaning to our meeting.

FABIO

Sure! I have not battled through this
chaos for nothing!

KOA

As you can see, Fabio, Tarra is in the
midst of a great chaos and needs
stabilising. We are conducting a
global project to save it and usher in
a new era for all of us. Would you like
to participate in singing together with
six other voices from the remaining
six continents in order to achieve
that goal?

That is what we believe is the
suggestion of the mysterious Golden
Tablet that my father discovered in
our garden. Here is the copy of what
is on that Tablet. Can you read it?

Koa shows him paper with the Tablet's contents on it.

Fabio takes it in his hands.

FABIO

Yes, I can. I also see the musical
notes in the form of triangles. They
surround a hexagon here, which
symbolises Tarra because our
entire planet is a story of hexagonal
rendering.

KOA

It is.

FABIO

I will do everything to help Tarra – it
is my home. If we do not try, how
could we know whether it will help?

Please, count on me. Have you found another 6 people?

KOA

Not yet.

FABIO

Would you mind if I join you in searching for them? I would love to help!

KOA

Why not – if you are ready to jump in my pyramobile and fly to other continents?

FABIO

I have already told you that I would do everything to help Tarra, and I meant that.

He makes a short pause.

FABIO (CONT'D)

What is the next continent?

KOA

Continent 5.

84.   INT. OMNIA – DAY

Omnia is flying to Continent 5 with Koa, Fabio, Huma, Rory and Romy, on board.

Through the window they see the green Continent 4 staying behind them and the multi-coloured Continent 5 approaching them.

FABIO

Koa, do you know something? I am not afraid of this chaos.

KOA

I can sense that in you. That is why we are together now.

Both smile.

FABIO

It might seem odd to you, but I was dreaming of something big happening so that Tarra transcends the lifestyle of SOCIAL SECLUSION. What really puzzles me is that the isolation seems to come as a result of the free choice of each individual and household.

KOA

Maybe it just SEEMS like a free choice. It could also be a design attribute of this civilization – a PROGRAMME.

FABIO

Do you think this programme cannot change?

KOA

Hmm... a fresh mind can conceive of
a life beyond the current programme.
One original thought is enough to
start a snowball rolling and create a
new reality.

*Huma silently relocates. Both Koa and Fabio observe
its short trajectory.*

FABIO

Yes. Programmes are nested within
programmes; REALITIES are nested
within realities. Discovering you and
the Golden Tablet has opened a new
programme in my life.

KOA

The Golden Tablet is a planetary
programme that activates smaller
and necessary programmes.

In that chain of small events, we
are preparing the ground for a big
CHANGE.

FABIO

Can we speed up the change?

KOA

Yes, if we stop talking and focus
on finding a volunteer in the next
continent.

They smile.

KOA (CONT'D)

Here we are! Continent 5.

85.   EXT. CONTINENT 5, CENTRAL SQUARE – DAY

Koa and Fabio carry one cat each. With an effort, move through a busy street. Many colours all around.

Huma flies above them.

People are dressed in the robes of various colours.

FABIO

Koa, what is going on here? Different colours are everywhere? So unlike my continent overwhelmed by green!

KOA

Yes, that has been the characteristic of Tarra so far: each continent dominated by a single colour, except this one.

But, the future may bring colours to all continents!

FABIO

That will be something!

KOA

I have an idea. Let us go to the Central Monument!

They speed up their walking pace.

86.   EXT. CONTINENT 5, CENTRAL SQUARE – DAY

Two males are sitting on a bench that Koa and Fabio are passing by. The body language of the two seated males reveals nothing but lifelessness.

A better look around reveals similar apathy in other people, who are either passing by, standing, sitting or talking to one another.

We follow a conversation of the two males on the bench. Their dialogue is slow, their gazes almost static. It seems a great effort is required to conceive a single thought and utter it.

Every sentence is finished with a significant pause, as if announcing the end of the dialogue. It is not clear whether they are great listeners or use silence to disguise their inner struggle.

PERSON 1

Good day.

PERSON 2

Is it really good?

PERSON 1

Depends what you compare it with.

An extended pause of a seemingly disengaged mind.

PERSON 1 (CONT'D)

How are you doing these days?

PERSON 2

I am not sure. Life, as I know it, is not
here anymore. It is like a dream...
I have started to wonder whether

what I am experiencing now is
perhaps also a dream, an illusion.

Another long pause that promises nothing.

PERSON 2 (CONT'D)

How about you?

PERSON 1

I do not understand what is going on,
yet I am very sure that something big
drives life in this direction. Whether
that direction is good – I would not
know.

PERSON 2

Does it bother you?

PERSON 1

It does.

PERSON 2

Why?

PERSON 1

Because, on a personal level, I cannot
plan anything, neither complete
any activity... It is as if something is
continuously disorienting me, and
the usual meanings are escaping...
I think, I am giving up on chasing
them. Does this make sense?

PERSON 2

Yes.

PERSON 1

Why?

PERSON 2

Because, more or less I feel the same. I lost my inner peace and do not have a clue how to restore it. No previous type of activity satisfies me.

PERSON 1

Do you, perhaps, have a solution?

PERSON 2

The only trace of meaning that I find is in doing what I am doing right now: surrendering to the flow while sharing my presence with others, whoever they are...

Their MERE BEING supports something inside me and keeps me going – at least for a while.

PERSON 1

How about all of us on Tarra? Where does this lead?

PERSON 2

Whenever I ask those questions, I become more anxious. Various scenarios pop-up in my mind. So far I have managed to end such episodes by convincing myself that Tarrans are benevolent and diligent people and as such do not deserve to be wiped out – therefore they should not be.

PERSON 1

You rely on Celestial Justice!

PERSON 2

Why would I not? It is just an application of the Universal Laws. Tarrans cannot be exempt from it. I pray never to forget it.

PERSON 1

I am not sure in it. I am not sure in anything anymore.

Person 2 very slowly gets up from the bench, ready to move on.

PERSON 2

Good day to you!

PERSON 1

Is it really good?

PERSON 2

Yes – if you want it to be.

PERSON 1

(most genuinely)

Really?

PERSON 2

Just think that it can always be worse.

PERSON 1

That will make me more worried?

PERSON 2

You decide.

87. EXT. CONTINENT 5, CENTRAL MONUMENT –
     DAY

Koa, Fabio and the animals arrive at the Central Monument which features the Tarran globe.

Koa carefully places the Golden Triangle around Huma's neck and directs Huma to perch at the top of the globe's axis where the Tarran flag is.

As the bird reaches programmed destination, it starts singing.

Koa and Fabio sit on one of the many benches around the Monument. Each holds one cat in their lap.

88. EXT. CONTINENT 5, CENTRAL MONUMENT –
     DAY

With a visible determination, a young tall female dressed in multi-coloured clothes (SOLAR, late 20s) is clearing a path through the dense crowd.

As she eventually emerges from the crowd, her eyes immediately latch on to Koa and Fabio seated on the bench.

Huma descends to Koa's shoulder.

Koa takes the Golden Triangle from Huma's neck and quickly puts it into his pocket.

By then, Solar is standing in front of them, without hiding her excitement as if she has just completed mission impossible. She is certain that a reward follows.

SOLAR

Hi, you might be surprised to hear, but I felt like I was being pulled with an invisible force through the whole crowd, without even knowing why I am walking in the direction I was taking. Actually, I knew, it was the direction of the pull.

KOA

Hi, my name is Koa. This is Fabio.

SOLAR

Hi! Sorry. I forgot to introduce myself. I am Solar. Nice to meet you.

She stops talking for a while, as if thinking how to continue the conversation.

KOA

Solar, you might still be puzzled why you hurried so much just to meet two ordinary guys and their animal friends.

He takes Huma from his shoulder and puts it on his left palm, then stretches that hand towards Solar to introduce the toy.

KOA (CONT'D)

Huma, can you please introduce yourself to Solar?

134

HUMA

Hello, Solar. My name is Huma.

Then, Huma starts singing a tune best suited to Solar's frequency. She thoroughly enjoys it. After a while:

FABIO

I will keep Huma, while Koa explains
to you the real reason for this
meeting. At least, what Koa and I
believe it is.

Fabio takes Huma.

The cute bird continues singing, thus camouflaging to some extent the background noise of the busy Central Square.

SOLAR

(looking and pointing to the cats)

Don't you also want to introduce me
to these two most cute sweeties?

KOA

Sure. These are Rory and Romy – my
personal guards.

He smiles.

KOA (CONT'D)

Obviously, they are not from Tarra,
yet they can function here.

Solar strokes both cats, enjoying their presence.

SOLAR

How did you get them here?

KOA

I visited their planet in my dream and
now they are returning that visit.

All smile.

*Huma adjusts its tune to contribute better to the
ongoing joyfulness.*

KOA (CONT'D)

As you can see, Solar, our planet is
experiencing a great chaos and needs
help.

We are preparing a global project to
save it, and to start a way of living
in a greater harmony than what
we used to have. Would you like to
represent your continent in singing
together with six other voices from
the remaining continents?

That ceremony will stabilise the
magnetic field of the planet and raise
its frequency.

SOLAR

You are saying that the combined
sound frequency will do such a big
job, just by a mere singing of one
person on each continent! What
makes you think that way?

KOA

I understand your concern. If
somebody presents to me that idea,
most likely I would ask the same
question.

SOLAR

I did not say it to oppose you. I just
used my logic.

KOA

May I show you something?

SOLAR

Of course.

*Koa opens the paper copy of the Tablet's content that
was in his pocket, and shows it to Solar.*

KOA

Can you read what is on this paper?

SOLAR

Yes. I can. Why would I not be able
to?

She looks at it interestedly and reads quietly.

Only Koa can hear her voice.

KOA

This is the copy of what is on the
Golden Tablet that my father dug up
in our garden. We strongly believe
that the Tablet indicates a real event
and suggests a solution. As the
situation on the planet is spiralling
out of control, we need no further
proof of this prophecy.

SOLAR

I see.

Solar is quiet for a while.

FABIO

Look, Solar! Koa is presenting you
something that might not resonate
with you. We understand. Feel free
to act as your essence guides you.

*While Fabio is talking, Koa folds the Tablet' paper copy
and returns it to his pocket.*

*Then, he takes the Golden Triangle from another
pocket and puts it around his neck.*

*Even though Solar is looking at Fabio talking, the
moment the Golden Triangle is out of Koa's pocket*

Solar turns her head towards the golden object.

SOLAR

What is that? A triangle? Is it perhaps
a part of the Golden Tablet story?

KOA

Yes. Your intuition is spotless. This
small Golden Triangle is a powerful
energy and communication device
and will be used in the solfeggio
ceremony. The ceremony is not
based on wishful thinking, but on
physics.

As Fabio said, please feel no pressure
while making your decision. Whether
it will be you, or somebody else, we
will be here until we find a volunteer
for this continent. Then, we will
go to Continent 6 to identify their
representative.

SOLAR

Can I have a few minutes. By the way,
when is the ceremony?

KOA

Sure, take your time. The ceremony
is tomorrow at 13:13. You will sing
inside this Central Pyramid.

SOLAR

The whole story would sound surreal,
if this chaos and confusion did not
emerge on Tarra. I am not aware of
any other project to save the planet,
but this one. So, I HAVE to join you.

I accept your invitation and thank
you for what you are doing.

FABIO

That is so great, Solar. Together we
are stronger. I already feel it.

KOA

How about finding a quiet place to
explain the plan in more detail?

SOLAR

Oh, yes! I know a nice place nearby.

89. EXT. CONTINENT 5, CENTRAL SQUARE – DAY

*Solar (holding Rory), Koa (with Huma) and Fabio
(holding Romy) walk through the Central Square.*

Not far from them are three Milo operatives, who eventually manage to notice Koa and his company in the crowd. Koa and his friends are not aware of them.

Huma utters an unpleasant sound as it recognises the Milo's frequency.

Alerted, Koa is not surprised when invited into conversation.

MILO OPERATIVE 1

Young man, can we have a word with you?

With Huma on his shoulder, Koa takes a few steps and joins the three operatives.

Huma starts humming.

Fabio and Solar are maintaining their own chat yet keeping an eye on Koa.

MILO OPERATIVE 1 (CONT'D)

When we met at our facilities, we advised you not to meet again – did we not?

KOA

Oh, hi! Yes. I remember. Can I inform you that I have not mentioned to anybody that you captured me and copied my DNA.

MILO OPERATIVE 1

Good to hear about your integrity.

KOA

Why are you then following me?
What are you trying to achieve?

It appears as if you might be working
against the Tarran people! Don't you
wish good for the planet?

MILO OPERATIVE 1

Of course we do. We love Tarra. But
what is good for us, might not be
what you consider good.

We were happy with life on the
planet as it has been from time
immemorial. Why change it? People
were content – were they not?

KOA

Why change? Living within the same
unchanging medium can be more
of a punishment than a privilege. It
does not facilitate evolution and the
unfolding of genetic potential.

Change is a sign of growth – though
sometimes slow, sometimes fast.
I would rather choose all the
distress associated with a change,
than endlessly live in a flatness of
certainty.

MILO OPERATIVE 1

Things are obviously changing on the
planet – this chaos announces it.

KOA

Yes, things are dramatically changing
and, if you do not mind, I would
rather do my own business than
philosophise with you!

As if he has just remembered something important:

KOA (CONT'D)

Actually, since it seems that the
planet is in danger of possible
catastrophic consequences, if we join
forces, together we could save it so
much easier!

MILO OPERATIVE 1

Why do you think it is in our interest
to save it?

We can evacuate ourselves from
Tarra in matter of seconds. Why
would we help you?

KOA

True, you do not have to, except
if you see the reason to exercise
GOODNESS. If that is far from your
values, and behavioural codex, so
be it. We will fight for the survival
of the planet without you, and will
appreciate if you do not interfere
with our efforts.

*As one of the three operatives talks to Koa, the two
others are busy mentally forming a triangular field to
engulf Koa inside it.*

We see a battle of the joint magnetic field of the three Milo operatives against Koa's aura.

Despite significant effort from the operatives, Koa wins.

His aura repels their mental energy and they walk away commenting.

OPERATIVE 1

I do not understand, we easily managed to disable his father.

OPERATIVE 2

I did not like that fluffy creature constantly humming.

OPERATIVE 3

But why did we attack him at all? There was nothing suspicious in his behaviour.

OPERATIVE 1

True. But he is exceptionally capable. So, it is a good idea to lower his frequency and therefore flatten his enthusiasm, just in case.

90.   EXT. CONTINENT 5, PARK – DAY

Koa, Fabio, Solar, Huma, Romy and Rory, are in a small colourful park. They sit on some grass in a secluded area.

FABIO

Is everything OK, Koa?

SOLAR

Who were those people?

KOA

I actually do not know them, but I met them before so they remember me. Yes, I am OK.

SOLAR

I did not think they had good intentions in mind, Koa, when they approached you.

KOA

You might be right.

FABIO

I was observing their body language.

My impression was that they were aggressive towards you, though in a clandestine way.

KOA

It feels so good to have companions that care. Thank you.

Imagine if we remain connected and share moments together?

SOLAR

I can. Actually, from not long ago, I have been increasingly thinking of a different lifestyle I would like to see on Tarra.

But who am I to suggest any change?
Or, how would such a change ever
manifest? Just because I want it?

FABIO

What change do you have in mind?

SOLAR

The people of Tarra are kind, and
there IS, SORRY – there WAS, an
immaculate social order on the
planet until very recently. However,
despite the seeming perfection of
our lifestyle, I always feel something
important is missing.

FABIO

Interesting you say so, Solar, because
recently I have also started to
resonate less with some aspects of
life on this planet.

It is the communication between
people – I do not mean those within
one family.

On our outings, when we meet
somebody, the traditional peak of
communication is an uttering of
"HELLO". If you are greeted with
"HELLO, NICE DAY" it instantly puts
smile to your face and YOU FEEL SO
GOOD. Only TWO MORE WORDS and
you are almost ready to jump in the
air!!!

SOLAR

Yes! True. Social communication on Tarra is superficial YET people seem fine with it. Or maybe they are not, but do not know to communicate their truth since they lack communication skills. It is a circular problem-solution relationship.

KOA

I am aware of all these Tarran traditions. However, I preoccupy myself with my hobbies and so am minimally affected by the fact that I live without a single friend outside my family. Faced with social remoteness, perhaps, that is exactly what others do as well.

Koa pauses while stroking Huma's colourful feathers.

Fabio and Solar listen attentively.

KOA (CONT'D)

I do not know how old you are, but not too long from now, when I turn 18, I will be assigned a specific daily job – as are all the adults on Tarra. It is not that I do not like working, or would like to avoid my duties as a citizen of Tarra, but I somehow anticipate that such a lifestyle is going to be monotonous and potentially depressive.

However, looking at the people on Tarra so far, I was NOT able to figure out whether they are happy or unhappy. It has been puzzling me. If they are content, which on the surface is what it looks like, then it must be ME who is wrong; OR TOO DIFFERENT.

I, kind of, settled with the theory that I come from a very different planetary culture, which is for some reason still vividly present in my cellular memory.

Whether that theory is correct – I do not know, neither do I object in case it is true. I am just aware of a certain incompatibility between myself and the frequency of Tarra.

SOLAR

I do not believe in coincidences. Koa, you are here to experience this incompatibility for some reason. Your presence on Tarra is meant to unfold through the frequencies you epitomise – even though you seem A BIT OFF!

She says that genuinely, with warmth and compassion in her voice, yet cheekily. As she finishes the sentence, all three of them start laughing.

FABIO

Off! Actually, all three of us seem off!

Solar, Koa and Fabio laugh more and more loudly.

We follow the impact of that motion.

People around the trio are picking up the frequency of laughter and spontaneously joining in. The laugh of three souls grows to the laugh of a great number.

A contagious laughing session spreads through the crowd like the flames of a fire, with Koa, Fabio and Solar at its centre.

91.   EXT. CONTINENT 5, STREETS – DAY

The three Milo operatives mingle through the crowded streets.

The wave of laughter reaches them yet they do not join in. Instead, they speed up their pace as if suddenly alarmed about a big danger. They rush in many directions trying to identify the emanation point of the laugh.

After much effort, they arrive close enough to notice Koa, Fabio and Solar (with Huma, Romy and Rory) sitting in a small park.

As they suspect that the laughter comes from Koa, their faces reveal an eagerness to do something about it.

92.   EXT. CONTINENT 5, PARK – DAY

Close look at Koa, Solar and Fabio. Gradually they all stop laughing.

SOLAR

Have you noticed what happened?
Our genuine laughter spread onto
others!

KOA

Yes, it seemed so contagious!

FABIO

What an experience! I've never felt like this in my entire life.

KOA

Same here.

SOLAR

Agreed.

As they are slowly settling back from profound laughter:

KOA

Thank you for these beautiful moments. However, Fabio, I am afraid, we need to move on to Continent 6.

FABIO

I am under your command.

He gets up quickly and salutes Koa in an elaborate pirouette. They all laugh.

KOA

Solar, I have no words to thank you for joining us. See you tomorrow at 13:00 hours, in the Central Pyramid.

SOLAR

I will be there. Good luck guys! Bye Romy, Rory and Huma. Actually, since

we will meet tomorrow, could I have
one cat with me until then?

*Before Koa even utters a single word, Rory walks away
from him and comes over to Solar.*

She lifts Rory up and strokes him gently.

KOA

Do I need to say anything?

Instead of any comment, they all smile.

Solar stays with Rory in her hands.

The others leave, disappearing into the crowd.

93.   EXT. CONTINENT 5, PARK – DAY

*We see the three Milo operatives watching Solar, who
is now on her own after Koa and Fabio left.*

Solar walks slowly with Rory in her hands.

The Milo operatives follow her. She is unaware of them.

*The operatives speed up and one of them catches up
with her walking pace.*

MILO OPERATIVE

It was a good laugh!?

*Disturbed from her thoughts and her beautiful uplifted
inner state, Solar looks at the face suddenly walking
beside her and talking to her.*

*She immediately notices the specific cap, and
remembers the person who asked to talk to Koa.*

Solar hides her uneasiness.

SOLAR

Oh, YES! It was. Did you laugh?

MILO OPERATIVE

I was too far from the laughing crowd.

Looks at Rory cat, pretending to be honest.

MILO OPERATIVE (CONT'D)

Interesting creature. What is it?

SOLAR

It is from the animal family known as CATS, not really specific to Tarra. But, obviously, they can visit planets like ours.

MILO OPERATIVE

Do you think I can hold it for a while?

SOLAR

If you really want to.

She stretches her hands offering Rory to him.

The moment Rory is transferred, the benign cat turns into a nasty little attacker.

We see Rory's "invisible" energy aura overpowering the aura of the operative. In this aura battle, the operative falls down and continues wrestling with Rory.

The cat scratches him and green blood leaks from his hand.

Solar watches this surprising event, as well as the two Milo operatives. Other people join the scene attracted by the unusual commotion.

Eventually, Solar interferes:

SOLAR

Rory, come! Come, come!

She bends down and takes Rory into her arms.

Back with her, Rory returns to the most innocently looking cat – cute and fully relaxed. The Milo operative gets up from the ground. The onlookers start to leave.

SOLAR (CONT'D)

I apologise for this, Mr...?

While composing himself and pressing the green blood leak:

MILO OPERATIVE

...Mr. KLAUS

SOLAR

Mr. Klaus, why are you talking to me? I do not know you.

Klaus tries to disperse Solar's suspicions.

KLAUS

Of course, you do not know me, as nobody on Tarra knows any more people than the members of their family. Do you think just because I do not know you, it is a good enough reason to never speak to you?

SOLAR

I am only referring to the social
tradition on Tarra.

KLAUS

Sure. I hope you do not feel offended
with this encounter?

SOLAR

I do not find it offensive yet, to be
honest, I do not see the point of it.
Why have you approached me, Mr
Klaus?

KLAUS

I thought you might be interested in
participating in an interesting project.
You are young. Life is ahead of you.
You could spend it in a different way,
more exciting than the life on Tarra
has been so far.

SOLAR

Life on Tarra might change, has to
change and is changing now! Don't
you think so?

KLAUS

Yes! It will definitely change with this
global turmoil.

SOLAR

What project are you talking about?

94.   INT. MILO UNDERGROUND BASE – DAY

Solar is laying on the same raised bed where Koa was, when the Milo civilisation was taking his DNA and body map for their Project Mélange.

A body scan is taking place. Solar is awake and aware.

The scanning machine stops.

Klaus is standing by Solar's head.

>   SOLAR
>
>   Where am I?

>   KLAUS
>
>   At a safe place.

>   SOLAR
>
>   How have I ended up here? Where is
>   my cat?

>   KLAUS
>
>   We only took you here. We did not
>   need the cat.

At that moment, Solar senses Rory's presence on her chest. She relaxes a bit, even though she is thoroughly shocked.

We see the energy of the "invisible" cat. Solar addresses Rory in her mind:

>   SOLAR (O.S.)
>
>   Oh, Rory, I feel you are with me. How
>   can we escape from here?

Klaus is still standing by her side.

SOLAR (CONT'D)

Klaus, you obviously brought me here, so I request you to return me to my place on Tarra.

If you do that, I am not going to ask any questions on why I am here and why you have scanned my body.

KLAUS

We can do that, but only if you answer one question.

SOLAR

What question?

KLAUS

What did you talk about with Koa and that other young man?

SOLAR

I am afraid, Klaus, I do not think it is anything to do with you. I am not inclined to say a word about it.

KLAUS

Are you sure?

SOLAR

More than sure.

KLAUS

Young lady, we do not practice torture to acquire information.

However, in exceptional
circumstances we have to.

Klaus moves away from Solar.

He walks towards a part of the room where two operatives work on computers.

As he reaches them, both operatives stand up and start chatting with Klaus.

95.   INT. MILO UNDERGROUND BASE – DAY

Solar gets up and sits on the edge of the bed.

At that instant Rory moves away from her lap.

It makes her increasingly distressed, yet she still appears calm.

We follow the invisible Rory. From Solar's lap, the cat walks towards the computers with Solar's body data.

We see Rory's mental power destroy the computer's data, while the two computer operatives are still talking with Klaus.

Rory walks back to Solar's lap.

She perceives his return and relaxes.

96.   INT. MILO UNDERGROUND BASE – DAY

Klaus is still consulting with his colleagues.

We only hear the increasingly dramatic music emphasising the tension due to the anticipated moment of torture.

The consultation ends. Klaus turns his back to the other two operatives who immediately return to their work. Klaus faces the bed where he left Solar.

She is not there.

97.   EXT. CONTINENT 3, STREET – DAY

Three Milo operatives mingle through the street crowd, not far from the Central Square.

This continent appears brightest of all, since the dominant colour is yellow.

It is very easy to spot people from other continents, as well as the grey-clothed Milo operatives.

> MILO OPERATIVE 1

> Koa's father is concerned with protecting Tarra. He is a highly suspicious person.

> MILO OPERATIVE 2

> Yes. That is why we are going to take care of him.

> MILO OPERATIVE 1

> It was not a big deal to harm him before. He does not have exceptional capabilities like his son.

> MILO OPERATIVE 3

> We shall be even more successful this time.

98.   EXT. CONTINENT 3, STREET – DAY

Tibar and Dora sit on a street bench. Rocco jumps off Tibar's lap and slowly walks away. Dora monitors him, then leaves the bench to get him back.

99.   EXT. CONTINENT 3, STREET – DAY

While Dora chases Rocco, Tibar is still sitting on the bench.

Under his robes, on his chest, Tibar can feel the Golden Tablet, placed in the newly crafted cover made by Koa before they departed from Dora's house. He occasionally touches it, as if checking whether it is still there.

The three Milo operatives watch Tibar. As soon as Dora leaves, they start coming closer to Tibar, but not to talk to him.

They are positioned at the corners of a virtual equilateral triangle. Their pace is synchronised, and the triangular configuration is continuously preserved.

At one moment, they take out a small pen-looking device and use it to emit certain energy rays towards Tibar.

We see those rays hitting strong energy field created by the Golden Tablet on Tibar's chest. From there, the rays instantly return to the senders, pushing them back. The harder the Milo people try to shorten their distance from Tibar, the more exhausted they become.

Eventually, the Golden Tablet's field repels Milo operatives and they leave after expending substantial but futile effort.

Dora returns to Tibar with Rocco in her arms. She sits on the bench beside him.

DORA

As much as people were interested in
Rocco, so was he interested in them.

While Dora is uttering this sentence, we see a man in xanthic yellow clothes (MIHA, late 50s) pass by in front of the bench.

The moments later, Miha comes back and addresses them.

MIHA

I felt some nearly blissful energy as
I was walking by this bench. I have
never experienced something like
that. My name is Miha.

TIBAR

Thanks, Miha. Do you want to join
us? There might be enough space for
you on this bench.

Tibar moves a bit towards Dora making space for Miha.

100. EXT. CONTINENT 6, CENTRAL SQUARE – DAY

Continent 6 is dominated by the range of dark blue colours.

Koa, Fabio, Huma and Romy, are at the Central Square of this continent.

We see them standing and talking to a young woman dressed in dark blue clothes (LAMU, early 30s).

LAMU

That would be great! I feel honoured.

At that moment, a greeting is voiced from behind Koa and Fabio.

SOLAR (O.S.)

Hi!

Koa and Fabio recognise the voice of Solar yet, in disbelief, they instantly turn back to check.

They see Solar approaching them with a big smile and in obvious relief. Rory is in her hands.

FABIO

Solar, is it you?

KOA

Welcome, Solar. You seem to have
been through a lot since we left you?

SOLAR

You could not be more right, Koa.

KOA

(looking at Rory)

Thanks, Rory.

At that instant Rory meows and jumps down from Solar's arms.

Romy follows by leaving Fabio.

The two cats on the ground greet one another with a series of gentle body touches.

FABIO

(addresses Solar)

This is Lamu. She volunteered to sing
for Continent 6.

The girls amicably smile to one another.

SOLAR

I am Solar. Great to have you with us.

KOA

We could walk to the Central
Pyramid! Afterwards, I will take you
back to your continents.

101. EXT. CONTINENT 2, CENTRAL SQUARE – DAY

*Tibar, Dora with Rocco, Miha, and RENNY (mid 40s; the
volunteer of this continent) walk across the yellowish
Central Square approaching the Central Pyramid. We
can see the orange tinted glass-looking top of the
Pyramid.*

*Dora walks by Renny, who is dressed in dark orange
robes typical of this continent.*

DORA

Thank you so much, Renny, for
joining the group of planetary
volunteers who believe that Tarra can
be SAVED.

RENNY

Thanks for giving me this
opportunity.

The group disappears as they enter the Central Pyramid.

102. INT. OMNIA – NIGHT

After finding and instructing Fabio, Solar and Lamu, truly excited, Koa is flying Omnia with Huma, Rory and Romy.

The cats are sleepy.

Huma is humming a relaxing tune, then he stops to inform:

HUMA

Continent 1.

KOA

Yes, it is. Thank you, Huma. Rory and Romy, you will meet Rocco now. I am sure you will all be excited.

Confirming meows come from both cats. They get up and follow Koa.

103. EXT. CONTINENT 1, DORA'S GARDEN – NIGHT

Koa walks towards Dora's house.

The cats recognise the house and start running towards it, leaving Koa well behind.

Before the cats reach the garden, Rocco comes out of the house and starts running towards them. Their reunion turns into a gentle wrestling on the garden grass with Huma circling above them.

Alarmed by the sudden commotion outside, Tibar and Dora rush to the garden.

TIBAR

> Look who is here! We have been
> missing you all!

Tibar, Dora and Koa welcome one another, watch the joyful cats for a while, then walk into the house.

Huma follows them.

The cats remain plying in the garden.

104. EXT. CONTINENT 1, DORA'S GARDEN – NIGHT

After a while, the cats stop playing. Together they walk through the garden.

ROMY CAT

> Is it time now?

RORY CAT

> Sure.

ROCCO CAT

> Off we go!

They disappear behind the bushes.

105. EXT. / INT. TARRA GLOBALLY – DAY (G-49)

G-49, the last day of Tarra's year.

The chaos, disorientation and confusion on Tarra culminate. Open spaces on each continent are full of people idly moving around.

We see the pyramids on the Central Squares. Inside: their huge walls are decorated with intricate geometric reliefs that also add to the acoustic properties of the building. Their transparent tops DISPERSE COLOURED LIGHT, specific to each continent.

It is 13:00 hours on Tarra.

In accordance with the Golden Tablet's salvation plan, inside the Pyramid on each continent one person stands at the central point:

Continent 1 – Dora, Continent 2 – Renny, Continent 3 – Miha, Continent 4 – Fabio, Continent 5 – Solar, Continent 6 – Lamu, Continent 7 – Tibar.

We see Koa TELEPORTING to the first six continents in turn. Within 12 minutes, he visits all representatives and places the Golden Triangle around their necks.

Koa then returns to the Pyramid at Continent 7, where Tibar stands holding the Golden Tablet without any casing.

Koa joins him, standing with the set of tuning forks.

106. INT. CONTINENT 7, CENTRAL PYRAMID – DAY

It is 13:13 hours; G-49.

Koa plays the La note to provide the necessary intonation.

Following the guidance, Tibar starts singing solfeggios.

We see how the Golden Tablet picks up the initial vibration, then reflects it hugely amplified across the planet.

107. EXT. / INT. TARRA GLOBALLY – DAY (G-49)

It is 13:13 hours.

Central Pyramids at other six continents – simultaneously. We see how the frequency emanated from Continent 7 reaches all salvation ceremony volunteers.

Tuned, they start singing solfeggios. We see the Golden Triangles amplifying the power of their voices.

We also see how the solfeggio frequencies impregnate Tarra's crystalline magnetic grid and envelop the entire planet.

We follow these frequencies. As they reach people, they make some of them stop on the streets and observe in wonder. Some begin to sing solfeggios spontaneously, unaware of how or why they are prompted to do so.

Immersed in these sound vibrations, people exit the frequencies of tiredness, confusion and depression. Signs of weakness fade away, being replaced by a growing freshness of body and mind.

Every minute the singing corpus grows and, eventually, every single citizen of Tarra is singing in unison and joy.

Triggered by the influx of new and uniform energy on the entire planet, all continents lose their dominant colour and are becoming alike. Foliage turns green everywhere. In utter amazement, the crowds notice these transformations and keep singing with an increasing joy.

The effects of the global energy shift also spread in an unexpected direction: on all continents, the top sections of the Central Pyramids (coloured yet transparent) start to open simultaneously.

We watch each of them unfold into a six-petal flower smiling to the sky.

After losing their strong hue, the petals of these architectural flowers turn into transparent colourless triangles.

Tarra's colour-dominated continents are becoming history.

108. INT. MILO UNDERGROUND BASE – DAY (G-49)

We see the three invisible cats gradually damage the Milo technological units, as they move from one space to another and from one piece of equipment to another.

109. INT. MILO UNDERGROUND BASE – DAY (G-49)

The Milo staff monitor the frequency change of Tarra's crystalline magnetic grid.

MILO PERSON 1

I do not understand what has happened? The crystalline grid frequency is not decreasing anymore. It is actually RAPIDLY increasing beyond our control. What could influence it so strongly?

MILO PERSON 2

Not only that, our other operational circuits are also being corrupted. Our technology is not working.

MILO PERSON 3

I feel dizzy. It is like a mental pressure of some sort.

A NEW staff member rushes in:

NEW PERSON

There is a fire in our storage facilities! It is rapidly spreading!

110. INT. MILO UNDERGROUND BASE – DAY (G-49)

The commander of the Milo Underground Base is in his office. He observes the entire situation unfolding on his screens. A sentence in red capital letters appears on the screen: "COMMANDER, WHAT DO YOU SUGGEST?"

He presses a button, and on the screen we see: EVACUATE!

In that instant, the sound alarm system is activated and emergency lights start flashing across the entire Underground Base.

111. EXT. TARRA GLOBALLY – DAY (G-49)

As the planetary solfeggio singing performance goes on, Tarra is being born into its new self.

We observe the intercontinental harmonisation of frequencies.

Continent-specific colours are spreading around the entire planet suggesting a civilisation with no boundaries between the continents or between people. The planet becomes an energetically integrated whole and ascends to an ever higher frequency.

At the very peak of the solfeggio ceremony, we see a cloud of aural bliss smash into the planetary energy ceiling and open the sky above Tarra that was sealed up to that very moment. Consequently, the sunlight on Tarra loses its milky property and a transparent daily light sets upon the planet.

The celestial realm embraces its child Tarra on its new existential coordinates. The long period of cosmic isolation ends for this planet, ushering in a different quality of life that is better suited for the next evolution stage on Tarra.

112. INT. MILO UNDERGROUND BASE – DAY (G-49)

Staff members hurry, preparing to evacuate their premises.

MILO COMMANDER

Do not forget to take the DNA sample data for Project Mélange?

MILO PERSON 1

It is already with me, along with the other essential data from this Base.

To reassure the commander, he shows him a pocket-sized portable device.

Immediately, we see the mental energy of Rocco destroy the data stored in that device. The Milo person is not aware of it.

The other two cats are gradually destroying the remainder of the equipment in the Base.

Alarm lights and sounds are piercing the senses.

Milo staff rush through increasingly dense smoke, boarding their spaceship in a hurry, and escape from their underground Tarra Base.

At the peak of the solfeggio ceremony, we see their spaceship exit Tara's South Pole.

113. INT. SPACESHIP MANNA-373 – DAY

After MANNA-373 witnesses on their screen the latest development on Tarra, a small number of the crew is gathered around Captain Urros and Faro in joyful conversation.

We hear an indistinguishable medley of voices. Then:

CAPTAIN URROS

Before I congratulate everyone on yet another successful planetary ascension, let us wait for some of our esteemed members to join us.

114. INT. MILO UNDERGROUND BASE – DAY (G-49)

As the Milo people leave their incapacitated and smoke-saturated underground facilities on Tarra, we see the three cats coming together.

Soon after they meet, they all disappear enveloped in a vibrating beam.

115. INT. SPACESHIP MANNA-373 – DAY

Following their disappearance from the Milo Base on Tarra, the three cats manifest in MANNA-373 and

*immediately transform into two men and one woman
(Rocco, Rory and Romy). They smile at one another.*

116. INT. SPACESHIP MANNA-373 – DAY

*Rocco, Rory and Romy enter the room with the group
that is celebrating Tarra's ascension. Immediately:*

CAPTAIN URROS

Rocco, Rory, Romy, welcome back!
It is my pleasure to congratulate
everyone involved in the project
"Tarra – The Golden Tablet-5" and
to pass the gratitude of the Cosmic
Union of Humanity to all of you.

ROMY

(looking to Rory and Rocco)

As cats, we very much enjoyed Tarra.
It is such a beautiful planet. May we
suggest that Tarra hosts a population
of cats?

CAPTAIN URROS

Sure, Tarra's sky is now opened.
They will need the protection from
the strong cosmic energy that cats
provide. It can be arranged.

CAPTAIN URROS (CONT'D)

*(addresses "old woman" who directly
worked on Tarra)*

Tyra, what will you write into Tarra's
Golden Tablet Number 6?

                         TYRA

    I have plenty of time now to think
    about it. Meanwhile, I hope the
    Tarran people will learn that cats are
    more than animals.

Vera finally joins them, slightly embarrassed and rushed.

                    CAPTAIN URROS

    What took you so long, Vera?

                         VERA

    I was on line with Koa, explaining
    how I have been communicating with
    him through my bracelet.

    He understands now that the
    bracelet is a personal devise for
    galactic communication, and I
    taught him how to access its video
    function. He was overwhelmed to
    see me congratulating him on his 17th
    birthday.

All cheer.

117. INT. CONTINENT 7, TIBAR'S HOUSE – DAY
     (G-49)

It is still G-49 day on Tarra. Joy strongly reverberates across the planet and is flooding Tibar's house.

Koa, Fabio, Solar and Lamu are in Koa's room with Huma. They are playing music together.

For a moment, Koa stops playing the keyboard to give a voice instruction for changing the internal walls' layout.

We see the huge wall units disappear into the floor. As a result, his room becomes a gallery overlooking the ground floor living area.

He returns to playing the keyboard with his friends.

The sound of their music floods the living room where Tibar, Dora, Renny and Miha are chatting.

KOA

(to Fabio, Solar and Lamu who are still
playing music)

How about if we plan to play music together in public?

SOLAR

Oh, YES! The Central Pyramids are ideal place to host any performance.

FABIO

That will be something! I am all for it!

LAMU

Exiting! I am sure the Tarrans are ready for such an experience, and will join in.

118. EXT. CONTINENT 7, TIBAR'S GARDEN – DAY
      (G-49)

Tibar, Koa, Dora, Fabio, Solar, Lamu, Miha and Renny are together in the garden. Trees are green, birds and butterflies offer multiple colours.

Huma is perched on the top of a tree.

In the background, we still hear the music that Koa, Fabio, Lamu and Solar were playing.

Everybody's face is shining.

TIBAR

DEAR FRIENDS, THANK YOU for following your inner guidance and believing in the seemingly impossible.

He makes sure his eyes also convey respect and gratitude to all his guests.

TIBAR (CONT'D)

I hope everybody has learnt something during this unique process.

For example, I have learnt that even being given access to a great external power, such as the Golden Tablet, I myself was not enough to unlock it. Because, I am rather insignificant as an individual. But, as a part of a collective effort, I am a precious component – like is each one of you. SORRY – each one of US... What a day!

He turns towards Koa.

TIBAR (CONT'D)

HAPPY BIRTHDAY, SON! And I believe
we are already experiencing what
you rightly hinted, by saying that
there might be more to UNITY than
what we knew on Tarra.

KOA

Thank you, father. Yes, with this new
frequency on Tarra, we will be able
to access new layers of meaning to
everything and to unfold our further
potential.

*Koa's curiosity never sleeps, revealing his unquenchable
thirst for knowledge – regardless of how much he
already knows. He looks around to everybody:*

KOA (CONT'D)

Still, why did we have the energy
curtains that were isolating the
continents and people of Tarra for so
long? Was it really only to provide a
clean research environment?

DORA

Not necessarily! The energy curtains
were also here, for as long as it took
us to learn the danger of separation
and make the necessary steps toward
global unity.

*From the tree, Huma descends to Koa's palm and starts
singing a birthday song.*

KOA

But where are the cats?

DORA

Most likely, where they existed
before they came to us. Happy
birthday, Koa!

EVERYBODY

Happy birthday, Koa!

Koa responds with a smile and a body gesture. He opens his arms wide up, looks to the sky and says:

KOA

Thank you EVERYONE and
EVERYTHING!

Then, he bends his torso deeply to honour the group.

All cheer back at him, then gradually disperse around the garden and the house.

Joyful conversations continue, strengthening new bonds.

119. EXT. CONTINENT 7, TIBAR'S GARDEN – DAY
     (G-49)

Tibar mingles through the excited group and stops by Dora.

DORA

You know what I have realised?

TIBAR

I have no clue. If I start guessing, it
might last a while. Please, better
spare us from wasting time.

DORA

I have realised that I now prefer
purple, as if I used up all that red
could offer to me.

TIBAR

This house will benefit from your
presence here and can easily
accommodate you – should you
prefer this ex-purple continent that
much!

DORA

You are brave, Tibar, do you know
that?

TIBAR

I do not know whether I am brave,
but I know that I love you, Dora.

*With both of his own hands, Tibar takes Dora's hands
and gently holds them for a while.*

*His love is pouring out of each of his cells while he looks
Dora straight in her eyes.*

*She gracefully matches this communication with a
warm smile loaded with endless love.*

120. INT. CONTINENT 7, TIBAR'S HOUSE – DAY
      (G-49)

*While the celebration is going on, Tibar approaches
Renny in the living room.*

TIBAR

Thanks for stepping in to help Tarra!

RENNY

It was not only my pleasure, but my
duty.

TIBAR

Renny, something has been
bothering me regarding your name!

*Renny is surprised by the mentioned topic, as if it is one
he would never like to tackle.*

RENNY

Interesting! Renny is NOT my real
name, but the one I adopted since I
was not fond of the name my parents
gave me. My real name is REN. Why
do you ask?

TIBAR

Let me show you!

Tibar leads Ren to the diary on his desk in his room.

*He takes the diary, looks through it, stops at a page
and shows it to Ren.*

TIBAR (CONT'D)

Everything in existence is deeply
INTERCONNECTED. I believe
numbers reflect that property of
life and was curious to check the
numerological background of our
solfeggio ceremony group. I used this
alphanumerical table.

We see the following table that shows numbers assigned to each letter:

1 – A, J, S
2 – B, K, T
3 – C, L, U
4 – D, M, V
5 – E, N, W
6 – F, O, X
7 – G, P, Y
8 – H, Q, Z
9 – I, R

TIBAR (CONT'D)

I calculated the numerical values of each of the seven names and wrote those values in brackets.

You can see it on this list, organised in the order of the continents.

We see the following list:

Continent 1: DO-ra (2)

Continent 2: RE-? (1)

Continent 3: MI-ha (4)

Continent 4: FA-bio (6)

Continent 5: SOL-ar (2)

Continent 6 LA-mu (2)

Continent 7: TI-bar (5)

As we watch the list, Tibar points out each name, starting from the top, and reads it together with the numbers in the brackets.

TIBAR (CONT'D)

DO-ra (2); RE-? (1); MI-ha (4); FA-bio (6); SOL-ar (2); LA-mu (2); TI-bar (5).

In other words, what we have here are musical notes:

DO-RE-MI-FA-SOL-LA-TI!

If we add the numerical values of all the names, which are the numbers in brackets, we get 22.

He points at the following short calculation and the number 22:

$$2 + \underline{1} + 4 + 6 + 2 + 2 + 5 = \underline{\underline{22}}$$

REN

It is a Master number!

TIBAR

Exactly! The number 22 is a very powerful Master number, which unfolds its power when goals transcend personal ambition. It combines the INTUITIVE power represented by the number 2 and the unique power of the number 4 to TURN DREAMS INTO REALITY.

REN

What about the question mark related to Continent 2? It seems you did not have a name with the numerical value 1! You assumed it was 1!

Yes. I did. See! The name "RENNY"
has a numerical value of 4 not 1.

*Tibar shows Ren the calculation related to the
numerical value of the name "Renny", which is already
written on the diary page:*

R = 9; E = 5; N = 5; Y = 7

9 + 5 + 5 + 5 + 7 = 31

3 + 1 = 4 (!)

TIBAR (CONT'D)

It means, with the name "Renny", the
sum is not 22 but 25! Since your real
name is REN, let us find its numerical
value!

*Tibar takes the pen, writes the word REN and starts
analysing, on the same page.*

*For each letter, he looks at the alphanumerical chart
to pick the corresponding number. Eventually, we see:*

R = 9; E = 5; N = 5

9 + 5 + 5 = 19

1 + 9 = 10;

1 + 0 = 1

When Tibar gets the resulting number 1, he underlines it.

TIBAR

Here we are! The numerical value of
YOUR REAL NAME IS 1!

*Then he moves his pen towards the list of continents
and names. On the line for Continent 2, Tibar writes
"RE-n (1)" by adding the letter "n", instead of the*

question mark, to complete the name. He then turns silent giving space to Ren.

REN

Why did you assume that MY real name might be different? Why not the names of others?

TIBAR

Why your name? Good question. I had to start with one name. Since you joined us last, I decided to check with you first. You could call this luck or higher guidance!

REN

I do not know what to say!?

TIBAR

The celestial system, which has granted you this body and life, coded you under the name your parents gave you. Therefore, the celestial system works with you through the frequency of the letters R-E-N, regardless of the fact that you have changed your name.

Tibar's words make a great impact on Ren. With a sense of renewed self-recognition:

REN

Yes! I AM REN!

TIBAR

I AM GLAD you are embracing your
cosmic identity on Tarra.

REN

Do I have a better choice?

*As they smile, Ren points at the list of the continents
and names.*

REN (CONT'D)

Look at those names and their joint
significance: DO-RE-MI-FA-SOL-LA-TI!

HOW LITTLE DO WE KNOW about the
way things work!

121. INT. SPACESHIP MANNA-373 – DAY

Captain Urros and Faro are reflecting on Tarra.

Faro is relaxed, except for his unceasing curiosity.

FARO

Captain Urros, what is the next
step in the evolution of the Tarran
people?

CAPTAIN URROS

They will be experiencing the
frequency of the next musical note
– until they have lived through and
assimilated frequency of all notes
within the ascending and descending
musical scales? And that applies

not only to civilizations, but to each human being as well.

FARO

I have to admit, I am a bit confused, because each continent on Tarra corresponded to one musical note already!

CAPTAIN URROS

That is true. But all those notes were different tonalities of a single note of the Universe of Music that charts the evolutionary scales.

122. EXT. TARRA, GLOBALLY, CENTRAL SQUARES – DAY

The conversation between Captain Urros and Faro continues.

We hear it, while we watch the following collage of synchronous activities on all Tarra's continents where a new flag is being erected.

Koa is on the Central Square of Continent 7, below the Monument with the Tarran globe.

He removes the old flag and attaches the new one instead.

Huma flies cheerfully around the ascending flag.

The fully raised new flag reveals six horizontal colour stripes, instead of five. From the bottom to the top: red, orange, yellow, green, blue and indigo.

The blue stripe has been added, while the purple hexagon in the middle remains.

People are cheering. The majority is still dressed in purple, while the rest wear other colours. The same applies to other continents, regarding their dominant colour.

On the Central Squares of other six continents Dora, Ren, Miha, Fabio, Solar and Lamu, are doing the same.

As each flag reaches the top, people cheer saluting the symbol of a new era on the planet.

FARO (O.S.)

Do you mind if I ask, how long
it might take for Tarra to evolve
through its new musical note?

CAPTAIN URROS (O.S.)

Maybe several hundred years or
several thousand years of their time.

Regardless, MANNA-373 will be
around to witness it, while we
continue serving in the UNIVERSAL
UNIFICATION PROJECT.

FARO (O.S.)

Is that unification project called the
Golden Age?

CAPTAIN URROS (O.S.)

Well done, Faro!

123. EXT. MANNA-373 – SPACE

A planetary view of Tarra, basking in a renewed sense of unity, freedom and joy.

Zoom out to include MANNA-373 monitoring Tarra from a cosmic vicinity. There is a geometric sunflower logo on the outer shell of the spaceship.

MANNA-373 makes a sudden turn, then speeds away through the silent vastness.

THE END

Published by
MILENA
milena@milena.org.uk

Printed by
Lightning Source, UK

A catalogue record for this book is available from the British Library

ISBN
978-1-909323-21-6